W9-ADN-971

And What of You,
nhine Ch

And What of
You,
Josephine Charlotte?

ELIZABETH
WITHERIDGE

And What of You, Josephine Charlotte?

drawings by Barbara McGee

ATHENEUM
NEW YORK
1969

W775an

*to the memory of the
unknown slave girl who was
the real Josephine Charlotte
long ago in Maryland*

And What of
You,
Josephine Charlotte?

chapter 1

JOSEPHINE CHARLOTTE sat alone in the grass on the hill where Master Robert's horses grazed. She was hiding in the warm stillness of the Maryland afternoon where cloud shadows patterned the rolling pasture and sunlight swept in shimmering waves over the green. It lingered on her dark hair and highlighted the gold in her bronze skin. She had come there to dream, but she dared not stay long. There were eggs in the basket beside her. Aunt Mattie had sent her for them with the admonition to "hurry, Chile, I needs 'em quick," but Josephine Charlotte was seventeen and the afternoon was warm.

When she was missed at the big house and Aunt Mattie's call came shrilling across the hills, she would snatch the eggs and slip back to the barns as swiftly as the summer wind. She would have to be exceedingly quick lest Aunt Mattie aim a stinging slap at her cheek. Miss Sarah wouldn't be there to stand up for her this afternoon. She had ridden over to see her grandmother at Fox Hill Farm.

Old Miss Martha was ailing, so Sarah had been sent with chicken broth and jelly for her. When she was away, the mistress or Aunt Mattie in the kitchen or somebody else around Uphill Farm always found something for Josephine Charlotte to do. She hated these chores because she felt passionately that she belonged to Miss Sarah. They had grown up together. Miss Sarah used to come out to the slave quarters, where Josephine Charlotte's grandmother took care of all the slave children, and coax her out to play. They would romp all over Uphill Farm until Grandmother called them in again.

She had loved only two people in her life, Grandmother and Miss Sarah, and now Grandmother was gone, dead two years and buried in the graveyard where slaves lay when they died. Josephine Charlotte scarcely knew her mother and father. They worked in the fields and came in so tired at night that they had little time for their daughter. Rumor had it now that Master Robert would sell them if he found the right buyer and the price was right. One thing had to be said for him, he tried to be decent about keeping husbands and wives together. If he sold one, he sold the other, too, occasionally even throwing the wife in at half price.

It had been Grandmother who really mattered to Josephine Charlotte. Her mother was back in the fields a week after her birth, and Grandmother had taken over her care. As a matter of fact, it was she who had named her in the end; no one else had bothered. At first she had simply been called "Sissy," but on her second birthday Grandmother picked her up and announced firmly,

"High time this chile be named. This one somethin' special, so Josephine Charlotte be her name, after Napoleon's lady. This baby goin' to be a fine lady, too. You mark my words."

After that she answered to Jo or Josie around the farm, but Grandmother always called her Josephine Charlotte.

"You wash yo'self, Josephine Charlotte," she would order, "and brush that black hair and hold yo' head up high."

Josephine Charlotte did, and she grew tall and very straight and slender, walking about the farm on her bare brown feet as proudly as though she wore satin shoes.

"Napoleon's lady be the Empress Josephine, now," Grandmother reported excitedly one day. "Hold yo' head up high, Josephine Charlotte!"

Now she sat on in the sunlight, hugging her knees and musing about her grandmother. How could that old, illiterate slave woman have known about Napoleon and his beautiful lady? She couldn't read, of course.

Who could have told her these things? Then Josephine Charlotte remembered that when she was a little girl, tucked in bed for the night with the other slave children, and there was company at the big house, Grandmother often was called to help serve the guests in the handsome, candlelit dining room. She must have heard them talking about a world far away from the farm in Harford County and stored the news carefully in her keen mind to dispense later to the children.

"It be a shame that you can't go to school like Miss Sarah and the other white children," she would complain. "You're smart. You should learn to read and write."

Josephine Charlotte did learn to read and write and understand figures, but to her sorrow she never dared tell Grandmother. Sarah taught her everything she herself learned at the private school she and her brothers and sisters attended, but she warned,

"Never, never, as long as you live tell even your grandmother that I taught you to read and write. We'd both be in terrible trouble if you did."

Slaves weren't supposed to be educated; it would be too hard to keep them slaves if they were. But Josephine Charlotte was "somethin' special" and Sarah loved her, so she took the chance. When Jo was twelve, she had moved into the big house to be Miss Sarah's maid, and then it became easier to carry on the lessons. They slept in the same room, so at night when the house was quiet, the girls had snuffed out all the candles but one and studied in whispers, sitting on

Jo's trundle bed, side by side.

Josephine Charlotte had learned very rapidly; in addition to being able to read and write, she had almost unconsciously begun to drop the slave dialect and talk like Miss Sarah. It was easy enough to hide her other accomplishments, but the speech soon became a habit; and when the colored people on the place noticed, they were scornful.

"Here comes her ladyship," they would sing out in high-pitched mocking voices. "Here comes Queen Josephine. Listen to her talkin' like white folks! Guess we ain't good enough for her no more."

"Josephine! Josephine Charlotte!" came a call drifting over the pasture from the direction of the big house. "Where are you?"

It wasn't Aunt Mattie's voice raised in anger. It was Miss Sarah's high light one, and Josephine heard a horse loping toward her. She was on her feet and back to the present in an instant. Sarah came over the hill riding Midnight, her hair glinting in the late afternoon sun.

"Aunt Mattie sent me for you," she greeted Jo. "She needs the eggs. Get on. I'll give you a ride back."

Josephine Charlotte picked up her basket and climbed up behind Sarah with a sigh of relief. Miss Sarah was here, so there would be no slap for being late. Midnight loped gently back to the big house.

"Mr. Harry's coming for supper this evening, remember," Sarah reminded her over her shoulder, guiding Midnight up to the horse block at the kitchen door.

Josephine Charlotte slid off and raced for the door with her eggs. A small black boy ran up to take the horse and help Sarah down. In a few minutes the girls were safely inside Sarah's room with the door shut.

"Help me take off this riding habit," she panted, unbuttoning the heavy jacket. "I'm just boiling!"

Josephine helped her out of the long skirt and the high laced boots. Then she poured cool water into the bowl and bathed her mistress' hot face. Sarah sighed in contentment and lay down on the high four-poster bed. She closed her blue eyes for a moment, but then they flew open again.

"Jo, I hope it's going to be a *pretty* night, full moon and all!"

"Why?" asked Josephine Charlotte absently, emptying the washbasin.

Sarah sat up on the bed and stared at her.

"Well, honestly!" she exclaimed. "Do I have to explain it in words of one syllable? I told you Mr. Harry is coming for supper, remember?"

Josephine Charlotte did. She nodded and went on tidying up the room.

"Well," Sarah continued, "put two and two together! I want it to be nice because he's coming and we'll probably go out to the garden to get away from the family. At least I *hope* he won't talk to me right in front of everybody." She was giggling and blushing now. "Mama said he has spoken to Papa about me, and, well, maybe tonight is the night he'll speak to me."

8

chapter 2

Miss sarah flopped back onto the pillow, and in a minute she was asleep with her long blonde hair spread out around her. Josephine Charlotte sat brooding on the floor by the window, with a familiar anxiety surging through her. It was the nagging fear that had haunted her often since the first time Mr. Harry came to call. She remembered the night so well —a mild one in winter; soft snow falling in great starry flakes beyond the parlor windows, a fire burning on the hearth and mingling its light with the gold of the candle flames.

Josephine Charlotte, upstairs helping Miss Sarah

dress, had heard Jonas, the black house servant, announce Mr. Harry's arrival, and tiptoed to the stairs to peek. He was standing in the hall, brushing the wet snow from his dark coat, looking around with interest. As he stood waiting for the young ladies to come down, candlelight fell on his face so Josephine could see that he was tall and rather handsome, but in his glance as it rested upon Jonas she detected the same arrogant indifference that she found in the eyes of most white folks. It was the look that said, more clearly than any words could, "You're a nigger, and not quite human."

She knew the look well and saw it often at Uphill Farm. It was always in the eyes of the farm manager, Mr. Calcott, when he looked at the slaves. The look was in Master Robert's eyes, too, even though he was reputedly better to his slaves than most owners. Gentle Mistress Elizabeth had it also, but with her it took the form of a vague absentmindedness. Josephine Charlotte had the feeling that she never quite saw any of them as *people*. Only with Miss Sarah did Josephine feel that she was really another human being. Those shining blue eyes held nothing but the warmest awareness when they rested upon her. But now Miss Sarah was about to marry a man with "that look."

A cold chill had gone through her then, and the same shuddering cold struck her now in the heat of the late afternoon. Miss Sarah had been in love that winter night, and it had lasted all during the rest of the winter and through the long Maryland spring, and now in the full glow of summer it was blossoming. "I think he's going to speak to me," she had said, and now she was lying asleep, dreaming of her love. Josephine Charlotte could tell by the tiny smile that curved her lips.

An imperative rap came at the door; and when she went to open it, she found Willie standing there. He bowed with a sarcastic flourish and said,

"Aunt Mattie send her compliments and ask would your royal highness please to come down and help her to get supper?"

His scornful eyes traveled past her to the sleeping girl on the bed.

"My, my," he scoffed, "some folks sure has it good and easy. Missus see to it that I has plenty to do when she take *her* nap. Come on, Miss Biggity!"

He reached out to pull her from the room, but she whirled in time and slammed the door on his hand. Willie yelped in pain and stuck his nose back in the crack. Josephine could see his black eyes glittering in the dimness of the hall.

"You come on, or I get Aunt Mattie up here after you herself," he ordered fiercely.

Josephine Charlotte controlled her fury. She had despised Willie ever since the night a year ago when he had caught her alone in the rose garden and tried to kiss her. Now she drew herself up to her splendid, queenly height and said, as calmly as she could,

"You go on back to the kitchen, Willie, and tell Aunt Mattie that I'm going to be busy getting Miss Sarah dressed for the evening. You know she's expecting company. If Aunt Mattie needs help, she'll just have to find it elsewhere."

Willie snorted angrily and backed out of the door, slamming it behind him. Josephine heard him muttering to himself all the way down the hall. Sarah heard him, too, and stirred on the bed.

"Is it time to get dressed?" she murmured. "What was that awful racket?"

"Sleep a little longer," Josephine soothed, ignoring the last question. "What do you want to wear tonight? I'd better get out your clothes."

Sarah yawned and answered with her eyes shut, "My pale blue muslin, I think. Mr. Harry likes me best in blue. Let's put a blue ribbon in my hair, too."

She went to sleep again while Jo tiptoed around the room getting out the cool blue dress and the fluffy, lace-trimmed petticoats that went with it. She laid out the small blue slippers and the satin ribbon; Miss Sarah would look beautiful tonight when Mr. Harry came to propose. Moving noiselessly to the washstand to pour water from the big white china pitcher into the bowl, she resumed her gloomy meditations.

She didn't doubt for a minute that Mr. Harry would propose sometime that night in the moonlight. He had spoken to Master; and it was obvious that Miss Sarah was rapturously in love, so there was no doubt what her answer would be. Josephine Charlotte shook a few drops of the best cologne into the water. She should be so happy for Miss Sarah. Wasn't this what every girl, every white girl, lived for when she was nineteen? They would have a beautiful wedding, and she would go away to live with her husband. She would take her pretty clothes and the lovely linens Mistress Elizabeth was sure to supply from her generous stock. She would take her other possessions and settle them in her new home, but one thing would be left behind—Josephine Charlotte would stay at Uphill Farm.

The shadows began to lengthen on the smooth lawn outside the open windows, so she must waken her mistress. Jo stood over her and wished that she really did belong to Miss Sarah, for of course she didn't. She belonged to Master Robert; and when Miss Sarah went away, she would be left forlorn and alone at Uphill Farm.

"Wake up, Miss Sarah," she whispered, "time to get dressed for Mr. Harry."

Sarah drew a long breath and let it out slowly, yawning and stretching on the high bed like a sleepy kitten. Finally she slid off onto the floor and wandered over to the washbowl. She washed herself with the cool, scented water, splashing it leisurely on her bare neck and shoulders. Sitting in front of the mirror a few minutes later, she smiled up at Josephine, her long lashes still spangled with water.

"Make my hair especially pretty tonight, Jo," she coaxed. "Oooh, you don't know how scared I am. Feel my hand."

She put her small, smooth hand in Jo's, and it was cold and trembling. Jo had to wonder how this pretty white girl could be scared on this happiest night of her life. She began to brush Sarah's hair. She brushed with long, even, rhythmic strokes until it shone like gold, and then she pulled it up to the top of her head and tied it there with the blue satin ribbon. She dampened the curling ends and brushed them deftly over her fingers until each curl gleamed like spun gold. Josephine Charlotte stood back and admired them with her head tilted to one side.

"Now, be careful until they dry," she cautioned. "They're beautiful."

Sarah's older sisters, Mary Ann and Ellen, came in from the big room they shared, already dressed for the evening. They sat down and spread their skirts carefully around them—Mary Ann in lavender, and Ellen in pink dotted mull. Josephine fastened the last of Sarah's frilly petticoats and held the blue muslin dress over her head. Sarah wriggled gingerly through the opening and Josephine buttoned it up the back.

"My!" exclaimed Mary Ann with a tinge of envy in her voice, "you certainly do look gorgeous tonight. Just look at those curls!"

She looked at herself in the mirror and twitched unhappily at her dark hair.

"Why can't mine look that way?" she complained.

Ellen laughed. "We don't have Josephine Charlotte," she reminded her sister. "That stupid Prissy makes mine look like mattress stuffing!"

Mary Ann nodded. "Melinda's all thumbs, too," she agreed. "She just doesn't have the touch. Say, do you know, either you or I can have Jo when Sarah gets married. We'll draw lots for her. What d'you think of that, Josie? I'm going to ask Papa this very night."

Josephine Charlotte slid back into the shadows as

14

far as she could. She wanted to turn her face away from the sisters, but the careless smile on Mary Ann's face held an ugly fascination for her. She tried to murmur some sort of reply, but the words stuck in her throat.

"Come, come," Mary Ann prodded, let's hear what you think of it, Josie. Anything I can't stand's a sullen darkie. No wonder they call you Miss Biggity out in the quarters. You've absolutely ruined her, Sarah. She'll be no good for anything when you go."

Ellen shushed her unhappily. "Mary Ann, you should be ashamed. I'm going to tell Mama."

Josephine Charlotte drew herself up to her full height. Her hands were sweating and her throat was dry. Sometimes Miss Sarah had actually jumped between her and the lash, but this was different. No one spoke for a minute, and then Sarah's voice came into the uncomfortable stillness of the room.

"We'll see about that when the time comes, Mary Ann," she said with dignity.

Josephine Charlotte released her breath in a long sigh as Mary Ann, followed by Ellen, flounced out of the room.

chapter 3

WHEN MR. HARRY galloped up on his big bay horse just before suppertime, Miss Sarah ran to meet him, flushing to the edge of her shining blonde hair when he bent to kiss her hand. Josephine Charlotte went out to the kitchen quarters behind the house and found Aunt Mattie in a towering ill humor, with Willie nursing his bruised hand.

"What bring you down in such a hurry, Miss Biggity?" Aunt Mattie demanded, glowering at her, "Mistress want dinner served immediate. Everything got to be just so for Miss Sarah's beau tonight."

Josephine Charlotte decided not to reply but hurried to help her remove the meat from the spit in the great fireplace. It was a plump piglet, and its skin was done to a succulent golden brown. Josephine Charlotte's mouth watered as Aunt Mattie laid it on the big Staffordshire platter, handing her pickled crabs to garnish it with. Willie was set to mashing potatoes in the huge iron kettle, and Aunt Mattie hurried with the biscuits.

"Here, take this jelly into the dining room, Jo, and be quick about it," she ordered brusquely.

Delighted to escape from the kitchen and Willie's sullen face, she hurried into the house and the dining room where Jonas, resplendent in his serving outfit, high white collar, knee breeches with buckles, and long-tailed coat, was lighting the candles in the tall candlelabra. Their light shone warmly on the silver and the fine white china and the dainty summer dresses of the ladies as they came in to supper.

Josephine Charlotte went to hold the door for Jonas as he carried in the fragrant steaming piglet and placed it in front of Master Robert with a flourish. She helped bring in the vegetables; then she carried the gleaming silver teapot to the mistress, while Master Robert carved the meat and Jonas passed the plates. Between Master at the foot of the long table and Mistress at the head, sat the rest of the big family, waiting with strained, unnatural politeness for everyone to be served before they started to eat. Miss Sarah sat beside Mr. Harry, of course, Ellen and Mary Ann sat together, and all the other brothers and sisters ranged around the table—Elizabeth, charming at sixteen, sitting beside her mother to help with the tea, the three small brothers, Benjy and Jim and Corbin, whispering with their heads together until they caught a stern glance from their father, fourteen-year-old Martha charged with the care of little Robert the Third, youngest of the nine children.

The Mistress picked up her fork and instantly all the children swooped down upon their own plates. Josephine Charlotte passed the steaming cups of tea and then slipped into the pantry where she could keep an eye at the crack in the door. A buzz of conversation began in the big room. Mr. Harry addressed his compliments to Sarah's mother for the delicious meal, and Josephine Charlotte could hear her pleased little laugh. She thought Mistress looked unusually tired that evening; in two months she expected her tenth child.

"Here, take these in," Willie hissed in her ear, arriving in the pantry with a plate of hot biscuits.

Josephine Charlottte was delighted to return to the dining room, full of laughter and gay talk now. She noticed that Sarah was very quiet, her food barely touched. The lovely pink flush came and went in her fair cheeks every time Mr. Harry looked at her.

"It's been a bad summer for crops," Master Robert was complaining. "I don't know what I'm going to do, come winter. Got too many mouths to feed, with the tobacco bringing in about half what I expected. Guess I'll have to sell a few Negroes before fall."

Josephine shrugged off the master's words. It could be her parents he had in mind; that rumor had been about for months, but it would make little difference in her life since she scarcely saw them from one week's end to the next. They were still quite young and healthy, so they should bring Master a good price.

She went slowly back to the pantry, pondering his words. If *she* were to be sold, the thought suddenly flashed through her mind. If *she* were to be sold, after the way she had been brought up, after the way Miss Sarah had treated her, more like a sister than a slave, all of her life. Mary Ann's petulant words echoed in her head,

". . . Miss Biggity . . . absolutely ruined . . . no good for anything when you go!"

Master Robert had said, "a few Negroes." He couldn't have meant her, too. He *couldn't* sell her, not Josephine Charlotte, named for an empress, the girl who was "somethin' special." But of course he *could* sell her, why not, if he wanted to. As long as you're *owned*, you can be sold. Her hands were icy, and cold sweat began to run from her body as she huddled in the hot pantry. He wouldn't sell her; Miss Sarah wouldn't let him. He couldn't, he couldn't! Were the crops that bad? Master Robert had seemed genuinely worried. Who could tell? Miss Sarah would be married to Mr. Harry and go to live in his house. But Josephine Charlotte, what of Josephine Charlotte?

Willie brushed past her in the dark pantry carrying a tray of sherbets, and trod viciously on her bare toe. It was deliberate—she knew it was. She swallowed a moan and went limping into the dining room to remove the plates. Her face must have mirrored her distress, because she caught Miss Sarah's eyes fixed upon her intently. She forced a smile; it wouldn't do to spoil this night for Miss Sarah.

The last delicious bit of sherbet was finished, and the little boys sat on the edge of their chairs, poised for flight, their bright eyes fixed on their father for the signal.

"You may be excused, children," he said, and they leaped away from their places.

"Let us all be excused," suggested Mistress Elizabeth, looking very flushed. "It's so hot in here. Why don't we go out to the veranda?"

She rose from her chair, and the others followed. Josephine caught the significant little glance that passed between Harry and Sarah as they left the dining room; and when she took a fan to the mistress a few minutes later, she was just in time to see them disappearing into the garden, hand in hand, in the warm twilight, Sarah's blue muslin dress fluttering in the gentle breeze, her golden head reaching barely to his shoulder. Josephine went on her way around the corner of the house toward the kitchen where she knew Aunt Mattie was waiting for her to wash dishes. Willie was waiting, too, hidden in a clump of azalea bushes. He leaped out and grabbed her wrist.

"Not so fast, your ladyship," he mocked her. "You not gonna keep away from me forever; you and your high and mighty airs. You c'mere. I gonna talk to you."

"You let go of me, Willie," Josephine Charlotte commanded him furiously. "Go on. Get out of here or

I'll call Aunt Mattie!"

She struggled to free herself from his grasp, but her strength was no match for his.

"No use callin' nobody, 'specially not Aunt Mattie," he grinned at her. "Aunt Mattie mad at you. All you'd get from her'd be a great big slap. Miss Sarah not around to help you out now. You jes' got to listen to me for a change."

He loosened his hold on her wrist a little and she twisted free.

"All right," she snapped, "but you keep your hands off me, and you get on with what you want to say because I'm not going to stay around you very long. What do you want?"

She stood waiting, her head held high, her dark eyes flashing. Willie rubbed the hand she had shut in the door that afternoon and looked at her resentfully.

"I wants you to look at me as though I was *somebody*, not just the dirt under your feet," he told her. "I wants you to look at me the way a good black girl looks at her man."

"At her *what?*" Josephine Charlotte gasped.

"At her man," Willie repeated, a grin of satisfaction spreading over his face. His words had gotten to her.

Josephine Charlotte stared at him incredulously. "What kind of stupid joke do you think you're playing on me, Willie?" she demanded. "What in the world do you mean by such talk?"

"Just mean what I heard out in the stable," he said, watching her slyly. "Master Robert done tol' Mr. Calcott he got a great offer the other day, for you and me together, but the gen'man wants to buy us done said the deal was off lessen we was married, man an' wife before he took us. He seen us both an' he thinks we'd have fine young 'uns for him. But, we gotta get married first. Gen'man one of them religious ones, think colored folk gotta be married by a preacher, too." Willie puffed out his chest and an expression of unconcealed delight replaced the sly look on his face. He grabbed for her again, but she was too quick for him. Her numbed mind was beginning to function, and she turned on him in fury.

"Get out of my sight, Willie," she cried, trying to control her voice for Miss Sarah's sake. "Don't you ever come near me again. If there was no other man in this world, I wouldn't marry you. Don't ever forget that—ever, ever, ever!"

She whirled and raced for the house, running blindly through the dusk, only partly aware of the words Willie hurled after her,

"All right, Miss Biggity. We see about that. We see who decide what you do."

Josephine Charlotte went into the kitchen to wash dishes because she knew her absence would be reported to Mistress Elizabeth; but she moved as though she were in a trance, responding to Aunt Mattie's grumbling only in little stifled moans.

"What's the matter with you, Josie?" Aunt Mattie finally asked, her voice softening a little. "Don't you feel well?"

"No," Josephine Charlotte answered, her voice scarcely more than a whisper.

"Well, the dishes are 'most done; you'd best get up to bed," Aunt Mattie decided. "You lookin' poorly, Child. Go on, now."

Josephine managed a grateful little sound and walked out into the dusk. She looked fearfully about, but Willie wasn't there. She stood listening for a moment to the muffled shouts and laughter of Benjy and Jim and Corbin playing in the distance and someone singing a mournful air down in the slave quarters —other voices took it up as it drifted to her on the evening wind.

She longed inexpressibly for a place of her own to take her despair. It was truly despair that overwhelmed her now; in spite of her disdainful answer to Willie, she was panic-stricken. Suddenly she wanted more than anything else to cry, but where did a slave girl go to cry? Under other circumstances she would go to Miss Sarah's room and sob her grief into the straw tick on her trundle bed, but this was quite different from any other sorrow of her life. If Miss Sarah came in from her walk in the garden with Mr. Harry and found her crying, she would insist upon knowing why; and Josephine Charlotte wasn't prepared to discuss her trouble with anyone yet, least of all her young mistress on this night.

She began to walk aimlessly in the deepening twilight. This thing couldn't be true. Tomorrow she would tell Miss Sarah about it, and she'd understand and be indignant. She would tell her father, and Master Robert would punish Willie for his evil, lying tongue. On the other hand, what if Willie hadn't been making it up and the rumor he insisted he had heard at the stable was true? Goosepimples popped up on her silken brown skin. She began to run past the barns, down the lane, melting into the shadows of the privet hedges. She stumbled over the brow of the hill and threw herself into the sweetness of the dewy grass.

Josephine Charlotte was oblivious to everything but her own anguish. She lay full length on her face, floods of pent-up tears soaking into the rich Maryland earth. Gulping, shuddering sobs wracked her body, and she let them come, unchecked, alone against the hill where nobody could hear. She lay there a long time until at last she tried to still herself, to quiet the turmoil in her mind. This could not be happening to her—this incredible thing. How could Master Robert dream of marrying her to Willie, of all the slaves on his farm? Willie was so crude, so gross, so stupid, she thought. Her flesh fairly crawled at the thought of his touching her.

She lay still in the grass while the last pink cloud in the evening sky faded and the first stars sparkled in the deep blue. A great silvery moon sailed up over the hill and lighted the place where she lay. Somewhere a surprised mockingbird uttered a disturbed note. The song of lament from the quarters was ended. Josephine Charlotte fought for self-control, her shattering sobs finally subsided, and she sat up in the moonlight, wiping her smarting eyes with the hem of her long brown skirt.

Now she could think and try to plan for her future, once so simple and uncomplicated, and suddenly now as dark and formidable as the sky when a thunder-storm brooded on the horizon. At last, as the moon climbed high, and long black shadows crept across the gentle hills, she stood up and turned toward the big house. Her decision was made, and a strange calm settled over her; not the calm of the beautiful summer night. This stillness that pervaded her was more like the stillness that hung over the hills before a great storm ripped their peace.

Josephine Charlotte had made up her mind to run away. It might not be until after Miss Sarah married Mr. Harry and left Uphill Farm; but sometime before Master Robert had a chance to sell her, if sell her he intended, she would run away. She would bide her time and wait her chance; and some day when it came, she would run far, far from Uphill Farm and the loath-some Willie and the slavery that she now believed threatened to destroy her.

chapter 4

LIFE QUICKENED at Uphill Farm after Sarah announced her engagement. An evening in late July
was chosen for the wedding, and work began immediately on the trousseau. Most of Sarah's things would
be sewed at home by Josephine Charlotte, but the
wedding gown was to be made by a seamstress brought
out from Baltimore. Miss Minnie, popular with all the
fine ladies for miles around, would come to Uphill
Farm to stay as long as necessary. Sarah and her
mother and sisters poured over fashion magazines by
the hour, and often Jo was called in to offer advice or
settle a disputed point because she had a reputation for

extraordinarily good taste.

"I can't think where Josie ever got such an eye for fashion," Mary Ann said one day when they were trying to decide on a winter outfit for the bride. "Most Negroes don't know one color from another, let alone material. What a pity she's black! She could make a living in clothes."

Once again Josephine Charlotte had the familiar feeling of being considered an object rather than a person. Mary Ann talked about her as though she weren't even there. She flinched inside, but her face was composed as she said,

"I think velvet would become Miss Sarah best. Blue is her color; it should be blue velvet trimmed with gray squirrel, and she should have a fur bonnet to match."

Sarah spoke up quickly. "Oh, I'd love the blue velvet, Jo!" she exclaimed. "I can see it now. Gray squirrel would be lovely with it, too. Can I have it, Mama?"

Mistress Elizabeth considered with pursed lips. "We have to think of the expense, Sarah. The tobacco is so poor this summer. It seems to me velvet with fur would require a seamstress. It would be very handsome, though," she finished regretfully.

Sarah's lips drooped and her blue eyes lost their sparkle.

"All right," she agreed reluctantly, "but I have to have something new for winter because my old pelisse is pretty shabby."

"I know," nodded her mother, "but wool would be cheaper—just plain, without fur, don't you think? And

27

lined with wadding so it will be good and warm."

"That's right, I don't know why Sarah should have velvet and fur just because she happens to be getting married," Mary Ann pouted.

"Yes," sighed Ellen. "I suppose we'll have to have our old pelisses made over this year. I'd hoped for a new purple wool."

Josephine Charlotte noticed the distress on Mistress Elizabeth's face and the disappointment in Miss Sarah's blue eyes. She glanced sidewise at Mary Ann and asked,

"Could Miss Sarah have the velvet if I made it myself, Mistress?"

"Oh, come now!" Mary Ann cried before her mother had a chance to reply. "A velvet pelisse trimmed with fur, and a bonnet, and I suppose a muff, too. You haven't had enough experience for that kind of sewing."

Sarah flew to Josephine's defense. "She sews beautifully," she insisted. "I'd trust Jo to make anything. Don't you remember the lovely dress she made for me last winter? Such tiny, even stitches!"

"A simple dress for home is one thing and a velvet costume is another," Mistress Elizabeth interposed mildly. "Josephine could certainly sew it well enough, but it would be the styling I'm not sure about. How would it be if Miss Minnie designed and fitted it, and Jo did the sewing? That would save money."

"That would be wonderful!" Sarah cried. "You'd do it, wouldn't you, Jo?"

Josephine Charlotte nodded and went out to help

Aunt Mattie with supper. Willie met her in the pantry.

"Afternoon, Miss Biggity," he greeted her with a mock flourish. "And what, may I ask, have you been doin' with the ladies? Plannin' the weddin' dress, no doubt?"

Josephine Charlotte tried to slip past him, but Willie was too quick. He seized her around her slim waist and pulled her to him. She felt his hot breath on her cheek.

"You'll be sewin' your own weddin' dress soon, don't forget that, Miss Biggity," he reminded her. "Talk around the barn is that Master won't be a-waitin' much longer. He be goin' to sell us, man an' wife, to pay for Miss Sarah's weddin'. You didn't know that, did you?"

His black eyes leered down at her in the dimness of the pantry. Josephine twisted and strained, powerless to wrench herself free from him. She heard Jonas in the dining room putting silver on the table, but she struggled in fierce silence; it wasn't like her to call for help.

"Jus' you wait 'till we're married," he whispered.

Josephine Charlotte shuddered and raised her hand to push his soft, fat face away when suddenly she heard Sarah's voice quite near, calling her.

"Jo, where are you? I've been looking all over for you."

Willie released his hold, and Josephine ran out of the pantry. By the time she reached Miss Sarah in the front hall, she had smoothed out her dress and calmed her breathing. Her hands were still shaking, but she

29

kept them in back of her. It was a simple thing that Sarah wanted. She had a fashion magazine in her hand with a design they had found for the blue velvet pelisse. Actually it was young Elizabeth who had discovered it, and she stood beside her sister, waiting eagerly for Josephine Charlotte's approval.

Jo thought the high waist, the rolling collar, and the plain long sleeves would be just right for blue velvet, and she also liked the velvet hat with ostrich plumes that went along with it.

"How about that instead of the bonnet?" Sarah suggested.

"Oh, the fur bonnet would be so *smart*," protested Elizabeth.

Josephine Charlotte looked at her appreciatively. "Perhaps we could make the hat out of pieces of the velvet, and you could have the bonnet, too, for cold days."

The girls were delighted and ran off to talk to their mother about it, while Jo went back to the kitchen, avoiding the pantry for fear Willie might still be lurking there; but he had gone. She didn't see him again that evening except under Aunt Mattie's watchful eye.

Mr. Harry arrived soon after supper, as he did almost every evening, and he and Sarah sat out on the veranda with Mistress Elizabeth knitting near at hand. Josephine Charlotte felt sorry that they couldn't be alone.

"How silly," she thought. "After they're married they will be alone all the time. They must want to talk by themselves *now!*"

When Sarah had said a lingering good-bye to him and come up to bed, she was bubbling with excitement.

"Jo, how would you like to go to Baltimore with me?" she asked, getting out of her white dotted mull dress.

"To Baltimore!" Josephine exclaimed. "I'd *love* to go, Miss Sarah!"

"Mama says we must go to the city to shop for my things, and you are to come along because you're my maid," Sarah reported, "but I honestly think it's because she wants your judgment."

Josephine Charlotte hung up the dress and picked up the brush.

"Miss Mary Ann and Miss Ellen are going too, I suppose," she ventured, pulling it firmly through Sarah's mass of curls.

Sarah twisted around, her blue eyes twinkling up into Jo's brown ones.

"No, they aren't going," she giggled. "Mama says they can't go this time because there won't be room in the carriage for all of us, especially coming home with Miss Minnie and all our packages. They'll be furious; they haven't heard the bad news yet, but Mama says they can go in later in the summer after I'm married. It'll be a real nice treat for them, she thinks."

"Mmmm," Jo murmured, "too bad they can't go."

"That was an out-and-out fib, Jo!" Sarah exclaimed. "You don't have to be so polite about them, just because they're my sisters. Mary Ann has been hateful to you lately, and you know it. Ellen isn't quite so bad, but even she can be nasty once in a while. I don't know what's gotten into them. They've never been like this before."

Josephine finished the brushing and began to weave the hair into two thick braids for bed.

"That's not hard to figure out," she said quietly, "because, after all, you're their little sister and you're being married before they're even promised. It makes them edgy, but I'm sure their turn will come soon. They're both so pretty."

Sarah went to the window in her long white cotton gown and knelt beside it with her arms on the sill, looking dreamily out at the clear sky, glittering with stars and bright with the moon.

"Sometimes you just plain discourage me, Jo," she sighed. "You're two years younger than I am, but you can figure people out so much better, somehow. Your turn's going to come, too. You're so pretty yourself. No, I guess 'pretty's' the wrong word for you. You're beautiful, perfectly beautiful—so tall and straight and well, *elegant*. All you have is a few old dresses, but you wear them as though they were velvet. I can never forget what your grandmother kept saying about your being a 'fine lady,' Jo. Do you remember?"

Josephine Charlotte remembered. And unexpected tears flooded her eyes. A great wave of longing for the beloved old woman swept over her. If she were here now, she would know what to do about the trouble with Willie, but as it was, Josephine had none of her own people to confide in. At that moment Grand-mother's "fine lady" felt utterly bereft and alone.

"We have to find a beau for you," Sarah went rambling on. "There isn't anybody but Willie any-where near your age on our place."

She stopped suddenly and then went on hesitantly, "I don't really like him very much, do you?"

"Oh no," Josephine Charlotte shuddered. "Don't even mention him to me!"

Apparently Master Robert hadn't suggested her marriage to Willie in Miss Sarah's presence. Perhaps it was just all made up, after all, she thought, her spirits lifting. She dashed the tears from her eyes be-hind Miss Sarah's back and turned down the bed.

"That settles it then," Sarah cried, as she ran from the window and flung her arms around Jo. "I wanted to tell you some news I heard from Mr. Harry the minute I came upstairs, but I had to be sure about you and Willie first. Mr. Harry bought a new slave today to take old Jeb's place."

"So? And what's so exciting about that?" Josephine Charlotte wanted to know, pulling out her trundle bed and beginning to undress. "I thought you didn't ap-prove of slavery much. I thought you were glad Mr. Harry only has a few."

"Of course I don't approve of owning slaves; it doesn't make sense," Miss Sarah assured her, "but wait until you hear about this one! Mr. Harry got him from John Thompson who's selling out everything and going to live with his daughter in New York. Naturally he can't take his slaves with him."

"Naturally not," said Josephine Charlotte, dryly.

"Well!" Miss Sarah hurried on, "He's *young*, Jo, and Harry says he's the handsomest Negro he's ever seen. John Thompson had him for a house servant—really sort of a companion, and he couldn't say enough nice things about him. He even taught him to read and write; and Jo, I had to bite my tongue to keep from telling him you could read and write, too, but I thought it best to keep the secret. Harry was so funny when he told me about him. He said, 'Sarah, I don't know whether I've done the right thing or not. It makes a man downright uneasy to have a slave that's maybe smarter than he is himself! He looks at me with those big, dark eyes and I don't know what he's thinking.' "

"Very funny," Josephine agreed, "but what has this marvel to do with me?"

"Stupid!" sighed Sarah, climbing up into her high bed. "What were we just talking about? A boy for you, remember? You'd make a wonderful pair! Now, don't turn up your nose at him until you've seen him, at least."

"All right," Josephine promised, "but don't forget, you haven't seen him either. Sounds rather unlikely to me. What did you say his name is?"

"I didn't say," giggled Miss Sarah, rolling over to go to sleep. "You can just wait a while to find out, Miss Biggity!"

chapter 5

T HE SOFT June days, perfumed with roses and gilded with sunshine, flew by. There was still an unbelievable amount of sewing to be done. Some of the other slave women were pressed into service to sew the miles of hems into sheets and table linens and towels, but only Josephine Charlotte with her dextrous, quicksilver fingers could sew the exquisite underthings that were going into the trousseau. Miss Sarah would let no one else touch the delicate cotton; no one but Jo could embroider the dainty designs and monograms.

Jo was so deeply involved in Sarah's wedding that she was able to forget her own problems most of the time. Only occasionally when someone reminded her how little time remained did she remember Willie's terrifying remark: "He be goin' to sell us, man an' wife, to pay for Miss Sarah's weddin'." She would shudder and hurry on with the tiny, perfect stitches. She tried to shut the whole revolting thing out of her mind, but she realized that she should be making plans. With all the excitement bubbling around her she couldn't seem to think about it.

During some of the rare moments when she was alone, she'd remember the old colored man called Richard Harris, who lived near the Susquehanna River and helped escaping slaves across in his small rowboat. Many times she had heard the Negroes at Uphill Farm talk about him, but she had never paid attention to where he lived or how to get there, never dreaming that she would ever seek his help. She would just have to trust to luck that if the moment came she would be able to find him.

Plans were going ahead for the trip to Baltimore, and even her big private worry couldn't keep Josephine Charlotte from enjoying it. She had never been out-side of Harford County, so traveling with the mistress and Miss Sarah in the carriage to see the city would be a real adventure. And there would be the shopping; she would be allowed to go along to carry the parcels so she could see the big stores with all the beautiful things there were to buy. Sarah was making a list of what she must take along. They would be gone a week, counting the two days enroute.

"I'll take that plain dark blue cotton to wear shopping," she said, "and my black leather slippers to go with it. I'll need two or three petticoats and camisoles, and, of course, stockings. I'd better take the white muslin and the pink one for evenings, and don't let's forget the hair bows and sashes that go with them."

She diddled with her slate pencil and thought for a minute.

"I don't know," she finally resumed, "whether two dresses for evening will be enough or not. Mama says that even though Uncle Corbin isn't married, he entertains a lot and everybody always dresses for dinner at his house. It's *dinner* at night, Jo, not supper like we have."

"Why not take the lavender lawn?" Josephine suggested. "That will do for afternoon, too. You might be invited for tea somewhere, you know."

They were going to visit Sarah's Uncle Corbin who was a doctor and a business man, whom Sarah called, "my rich uncle."

Sarah wrote down "lavender lawn" and sat swinging her foot and pondering. Suddenly she whirled to Josephine and cried,

"Now we have to think about you. What're *you* going to take, Jo?"

Josephine Charlotte laid down her sewing with a wry little grin.

"Well," she said slowly, checking on her fingers, "let's see now. Why don't I take my brand new silk bombazine, and the yellow muslin and last summer's green lawn, and oh, I have so many to choose from, I just can't decide!"

"Jo, now you're being sarcastic," moaned Sarah. "It was silly of me even to ask. I know you haven't got anything pretty, and it's all wrong, and it makes me mad, but you haven't and that's the way it is, and I can't help it. I should have asked, instead, 'What are we going to find for you?' "

Josephine Charlotte looked up in time to see Sarah dash her hands across her eyes, and she was all contrition immediately.

"My goodness, don't cry!" she exclaimed. "I was just joking. Who cares what my clothes look like, anyway? Nobody will be looking at your maid; they'll be all eyes for the bride. I'll just do up a couple of things and be all right."

"No you won't be all right," Sarah insisted. "You've got to have something pretty to take. Your clothes are a fright, and you know it. Didn't Mama give you cloth for a dress when she gave everybody the allotment this spring? What became of it? You never made it up, did you?"

Josephine Charlotte laughed. "No, I never did," she replied. "I forgot all about it because we've been so busy about your trousseau. It was a pretty piece of red calico, but there isn't time to make it now. I'll do it when we come back. Maybe I'll wear it at your wedding."

"You'll not wear red calico at my wedding," Sarah cried indignantly. "And you won't wear red calico to Baltimore, either. That's all right for around here, but not for Uncle Corbin's. We'll think of something else."

Josephine Charlotte resumed shirring the ruffle for a petticoat, and Miss Sarah doodled on her slate, her eyes thoughtful.

"I know," she cried. "You go upstairs and find that green muslin of mine. The one you always said made my eyes look green instead of blue. Mr. Harry doesn't like that dress, and I'm not going to take it with me when I'm married. Put it on and let's see how it looks on you. It might be just the thing, if it isn't too short. You're so slim the width wouldn't be any problem."

Jo put down the ruffle and ran into the house just as Miss Mary Ann and Miss Ellen sailed out onto the veranda, all decked out for a neighborhood tea. She found the dress and stripping off her faded yellow calico, stepped into it. It was a struggle to hook it up alone and tie the sash, but she managed, and stood for a minute looking at herself in the long mirror before she went downstairs. It was perfect—just perfect. Too short, but that was easily fixed. The soft, silver-green that had not flattered Miss Sarah did something beautiful to her own warm bronze skin. It made liquid pools of her dark eyes and a dusky halo of her curly dark hair. As she looked, an unwilling smile flitted over her face and she hurried downstairs to show Sarah. Miss Mary Ann and Miss Ellen were sitting primly in the porch swing, swaying gently to and fro. Josephine Charlotte tiptoed out onto the veranda and curtseyed formally, her eyes sparkling with the fun of the moment. Ellen looked at Josephine in silent disbelief and then burst into laughter.

"Good grief, what have we here!" she exclaimed.

39

"A fancy dress show?"

Josephine Charlotte was so taken aback that she froze into a lovely bronze statue, but Mary Ann jumped to her feet and confronted Sarah.

"What do you think you're doing?" she demanded furiously. "Where did she get that dress?"

Sarah was perfectly composed. "From my wardrobe, of course. What difference does it make to you?" she wanted to know.

Josephine stood silent, her great eyes turning from one to the other of the sisters.

"I'll tell you what difference it makes to me." Mary Ann fairly sputtered in her rage. "She has no business wearing a dress like that."

"And why not?" cried Sarah, a bright red spot beginning to burn on each cheek. "This is an old dress of mine and I have a right to do what I want with it; and I might add that it's no business of yours what I do with my own clothes when I'm about to be married. Harry doesn't like this dress, and I don't intend to take it with me. If I choose to give it to Jo, it's my affair and not yours."

"If you give a dress like that to a slave, it's the affair of everyone in our family," shrilled Mary Ann, walking up and down on the veranda.

"Why?" insisted Sarah. "I demand to know why. I looked absolutely bilious in that shade of green, and as you can see, it's perfectly lovely on Jo. Why shouldn't she have it? All she needs to do is let the hem down, and maybe fix the waistline with a wider sash or something. You don't want it, do you? It would certainly be awful with *your* sallow complexion."

Mary Ann stopped pacing to look at Josephine Charlotte and then she turned to Sarah, her voice still vibrant with anger, but now something else mingled with it.

"I know it's perfectly lovely on her," she admitted. "That's the trouble, she shouldn't look like that, Sarah. Oh, why can't you understand me? No slave should ever look like that. It isn't right."

Suddenly Josephine Charlotte identified the new mood she heard in the voice and saw in the eyes. It was fear that echoed there, and Jo felt sorry for Mary Ann. She looked down at the beautiful full green skirt with its fluffy ruffles and caressed it with her slender fingers. She looked at Mary Ann and saw the apprehension in her face, and at Ellen who had averted her eyes and was playing with the ruffles on her own skirt; then she turned to Sarah and made the most sacrificial speech of her life.

"Maybe it isn't suitable, Miss Sarah," she said. "I do love it, and I thank you for offering it to me, but I guess maybe it isn't right for me. I'll go and take it off."

"No, leave it on for a bit," Miss Sarah said. "You can change later. We'll talk to Mama, and she shall decide about it. I want you to have it, Jo," she went on as Jonas brought the carriage to the horse block and the girls departed for their tea. "Don't let Mary Ann and Ellen upset you. They're jealous, that's all."

Josephine sat down and began to sew the ruffle again with fingers that weren't perfectly steady. As they worked and chattered about the trip to Baltimore, a young Negro man came riding around the curve in the drive toward them. He was on a heavy farm horse that Miss Sarah immediately recognized as one of Mr. Harry's. She poked Josephine and whispered,

"That's George. I'm sure it is. Let's go see him."

"Who?" asked Josephine Charlotte.

"George, silly—Mr. Harry's new boy. Don't you remember?"

"You never told me his name," Josephine reminded her. "You go. I'm too busy. If I stop for every little thing, I'll never get your things ready."

George had passed the house now, with a polite nod to the girls, and disappeared from sight in the direction of the kitchen.

"I want you to come," Sarah insisted. "This isn't a little thing. It's important. You've got to meet him, and I want to myself. I'm really curious. Come on, Jo—it won't take a minute."

Josephine had to admit that she was a little curious herself, so she laid down her sewing reluctantly, unexpectedly overtaken with shyness. Sarah grabbed her hand and pulled her along the drive.

"Come on," she coaxed. She looked up into Josephine Charlotte's face and exclaimed, "Why, Jo! What's the matter with you? I've never seen you like this before. I do believe you're bashful."

Jo didn't want to talk about it, so she said nothing for a minute and by that time they were around the corner of the house and Sarah's attention was turned to George, who had dismounted and was standing at

42

the kitchen door talking to Aunt Mattie. Evidently he had brought a gift from Mr. Harry's garden, for Aunt Mattie was holding a basket of fresh vegetables in her hand as she chatted with him. He looked up as the girls came into view; and at first Josephine Charlotte noticed only one thing about him, a pair of the largest, most intense brown eyes she had ever seen. They flicked lightly over Miss Sarah and focused on her. She tried to look away, but found herself magnetized.

"You're George," she heard her mistress saying. "I'm Miss Sarah, and this is Josephine Charlotte. I expect you've heard Mr. Harry speak of Jo?"

George gave a courtly bow in Sarah's direction, but his eyes never left Josephine's face. After a desperate attempt she finally managed to turn away. She could feel the hot blood surging up into her face. Sarah still held her hand in a tight grip or she would have fled back to her sewing. Instead she stood in confusion, until Sarah twitched at her hand and laughed.

"What in the world is the matter with you, Jo?" she asked for the second time. "Aren't you even going to speak to George?"

Josephine Charlotte could tell that she was disappointing Sarah, so she forced herself to look at him again. Once more she felt the almost hypnotic effect of those intense eyes. This time she managed to get out a prim, "How do you do?"

"Very well, thank you," he smiled, "and how do *you* do, Miss Josephine Charlotte?"

She should have known that was the wrong thing to say. Miss Sarah, giggling, dropped her hand and went over to admire the vegetables George had brought. She would have to make her own conversation or stand mute under that bright brown gaze. His eyes were sparkling with amusement, and she knew that he was having fun with her, the articulate Josephine Charlotte. She would have to say something to break this silly impasse.

"I'm well," she assured him, feeling foolish, "but I'm very busy sewing for Miss Sarah's wedding, and really, I must get back to it."

She was suddenly aware that tall as she was, he towered over her, and she had to look up into the strong brown face. He nodded.

"Yes, it is a busy time. But you and I should know each other better if your mistress is to wed my master, don't you think?"

She did think so. Her lovely face relaxed its tight lines, and a smile curved her lips. George saw that he was making headway at last, so was quick to take advantage of it.

"This evening after supper may I come to see you?" he asked. "I feel sure that Mr. Harry would give me leave."

Josephine Charlotte's heart was beating fast. She felt the strange shyness overwhelming her again, but she pushed it away and answered him quietly,

"Not tonight because we're so busy getting ready to go to Baltimore. We leave soon for a week in the city," she hurried on. "We have to shop for Miss Sarah's wedding. No, there isn't time for any visiting before we go."

44

She could see disappointment in his eyes. Miss Sarah had turned back to them, and in a minute George would swing himself onto the horse again and be off down the drive. Unexpectedly Josephine found herself hating to see him go and very anxious to see him again. She tilted her face up to his and whispered hastily,

"When we come back, please!"

George bowed to Miss Sarah and smiled at Josephine Charlotte.

"Until your return," he said, climbing onto the back of his clumsy steed. "A safe journey!"

At that moment Willie emerged from the kitchen where he had been scrubbing the floor and surveyed George suspiciously. His small eyes shifted to Josephine Charlotte in her short green dress, standing beside the horse and returning George's smile.

"Well! And where might you be getting a dress like that, Miss Biggity? An' who might you be dressin' up for? That's what I wanna know," he bawled. His hand shot out to catch her by the shoulder, evidently unaware of the others watching him. George leaped from the horse and started toward him, but Sarah was quicker. She interposed her small body between Willie and Josephine.

"Go in the house, Willie," she commanded. "And don't ever let me see you try to touch her again. Do you hear?"

Willie dropped his arm and turned sullenly toward the door, muttering under his breath. George returned to his horse, the brown eyes still flashing, and Josephine Charlotte and Sarah walked back to the veranda in silence. Jo was still shaken by Willie's appearance. This was the first time Willie had ever threatened real violence.

"Let's forget him," Sarah finally broke the silence, "and think about George. I have never seen such a handsome Negro in all my life, nor such a polite one. He was all ready to come to your rescue, Jo. I almost wish I'd let him. It would have been the event of a lifetime to see him lay Willie out, wouldn't it?"

Josephine Charlotte nodded and moved onto the veranda with quiet dignity in Miss Sarah's lovely green dress. She sat down and began to slip the needle in and out, in and out of the petticoat, setting a row of precise, exquisite stitches in the filmy cotton.

"Well, what do you think of him?" Sarah asked, not able to wait any longer.

"What do I think?" Josephine Charlotte mused. "I think he's 'somethin' special!' "

chapter 6

"OF COURSE you'll take the green dress to Baltimore, Jo," Mistress Elizabeth said decidedly as they packed for the trip a few days later. "Mr. Corbin's servants are all well-dressed, and he will expect you to look nice, too. It's not too dressy for the city. I hadn't noticed that you hadn't made up the red calico. After Miss Sarah is married, you'll have time to sew for yourself. I'm glad she thought of the green for you; it's true, it never did become her. You make the necessary alterations and take it."

Josephine Charlotte's heart gave a joyful lurch, because she had been so afraid the mistress would feel

47

the way Miss Mary Ann had about it. If Grandmother could only have seen her in the beautiful green dress! She finished pressing Sarah's lavender lawn and exchanged the iron for another hot one in the fireplace. She would press her old brown gingham; it was shabby, but it would do for the trip, and she could wear it mornings in Baltimore. Miss Sarah came down with an armful of petticoats for her.

"You'll need these for the green dress," she explained, "to make the skirt stand out right. Oh, I'm so excited I can hardly stand it. I can't wait until tomorrow. Mama says we'll start at dawn, but even then it'll be dark by the time we get there, because we're going to stop at noon. Imagine driving into Baltimore in the dark!"

She twirled around the kitchen in her ruffled white morning dress. Jo applied a wet finger to the bottom of her iron; it sizzled.

"Hot enough," she said with satisfaction. "It won't take a minute to do these dresses, and then we'll pack."

Miss Mary Ann came into Sarah's room a little later and saw all the freshly pressed dresses hanging in the wardrobe, the green muslin among them.

"Hmm!" she snorted. "So Mama's letting you take the green one. I'm certainly glad I'm not going along. I'd be embarrassed. A colored girl wearing a lady's dress!"

So saying, she flounced out, and they could hear her stamping down the stairs.

"Sour grapes!" Sarah commented, dabbing at her

shiny nose with a powdered chamois skin. "Don't pay attention to her, Jo. Let's pack."

Josephine packed everything neatly in the big valise and put the toilet articles, hair bows and handkerchiefs in the hat box with Sarah's best summer bonnet. Miss Ellen came in to inspect the preparations.

"Hmm," she murmured," so you're going to take the green one after all, Josie. Well, I must say it's nice on you, no matter what Mary Ann thinks. What're you going to take for your feet? You can't go barefoot, and you certainly can't wear those clunky winter shoes you have for the farm."

Josephine Charlotte and Sarah stopped packing and stared at each other in dismay. Neither one had given shoes a thought. Slaves went barefoot all summer. Josephine felt crushed; the first pretty dress she had ever possessed in her whole life, and now nothing to wear on her feet! She stared down at them miserably.

"I know," cried Miss Sarah, running to the wardrobe and pulling out a pair of her small black slippers. "These will be fine; you take these."

Josephine Charlotte looked at the little black slippers and down again at her own long, slender feet, and then at her small mistress' earnest face watching her. She had to smile in spite of herself.

"How could I possibly get into those slippers?" she demanded, hating to see the look of disappointment cloud Miss Sarah's blue eyes. "My feet must be twice as long as yours."

"They are not!" protested Sarah. "Your feet are much more slender than mine. Try them on. I'm sure

49

they'll fit."

Josephine Charlotte sat on the floor and tugged, but she'd been right. She couldn't even pull it over her heel. She began to laugh and all of a sudden, without the slightest warning, she was crying. She stifled the sobs that rose in her throat, but the tears ran silently, unchecked down her cheeks.

"Oh, don't cry, Jo," Sarah crooned over her, kneeling on the floor, wiping the tears with a perfumed handkerchief. "You mustn't cry. I can't bear it. We'll find something for you to wear. Don't you worry."

"Well, my goodness!" Miss Ellen exclaimed crossly, stalking out of the room. "What a commotion!"

"I'm sorry," Josephine Charlotte apologized, snuffling mightily and getting up from the floor. With a great effort the tears were stopped, and she went to the basin to wash her eyes. The door flew open and Miss Ellen stalked back in, carrying a pair of black silk slippers. She thrust them into Josephine's hands.

"Here, take these," she flung out the words. "They're pretty worn out, but they're better than those clunky ones. See if they fit. My feet are lots bigger than Sarah's."

Josephine Charlotte hesitated, her eyes met Ellen's for a long moment, and then she sat down on the floor again and slipped her slim feet into the old silk slippers. They did fit, and she went on to tie the ribbons around her slender ankles. Miss Ellen stayed long enough to see that they were right and then left again, muttering as she went, "What'll Mary Ann say?"

Josephine Charlotte leaped to her feet and did a

few little dance steps, radiant now, with her long black lashes still spangled with tears. Miss Sarah seized her around the waist and danced with her.

"I never saw you cry before, Jo," she said wonderingly, "not even when we were little girls."

"I know," Josephine agreed, "I hardly ever cry. Grandmother taught me not to, but somehow I couldn't help it; it just happened. It's because I love the green dress so much, I 'spose."

The girls were up in the morning long before dawn, far too excited to eat more than a bite of breakfast. As the sun rose behind the hills, Willie carried the luggage out to the carriage where Jonas was waiting at the horseblock, holding the sleek black horses. The master was there to help them in and Willie gave Josephine Charlotte a hand up to the high seat beside Jonas.

"It won't be long now," he whispered into her ear, winking broadly at her.

Josephine pretended not to hear and busied herself adjusting her long brown gingham skirt around her. The sun thrust pale shafts of gold through the trees as Jonas clucked to the horses and the carriage moved off down the drive. Sarah leaned out to wave to her father, and Josephine twisted around on the seat to look back at the big house gilded in the dawn haze. Mary Ann and Ellen were leaning from their bedroom window, calling good-by. Josephine Charlotte waved back, hesitantly, to Miss Ellen, remembering the black silk slippers packed in Miss Sarah's bag. This was the first time she had ridden away from the farm in the carriage, and she felt very grand, sitting up there beside Jonas, rolling down the curving drive toward the road. As they rounded the last bend and came to the gate, two riders were sitting on their horses, waiting for them.

"Harry!" cried Miss Sarah. "What a surprise! I had no idea you were coming to see us off."

Mr. Harry dismounted and came to the carriage, smiling and bowing to the mistress and bending over Miss Sarah's hand.

"I couldn't resist coming," he said, "and besides, we have a present for your trip."

Then George slid off the back of the old farm horse and handed a small basket to Miss Sarah. It was heaped with golden peaches, flushed with pink, and the dew still on them.

"The first I've had this summer!" she exclaimed. "Simply luscious, and you just picked them, George."

"Before sun-up." He smiled, walking around to Josephine's side of the carriage to talk to her.

He was so tall that his eyes were on a level with hers.

"You look like a queen on a throne up there, Miss Biggity," he said softly with a twinkle in his eyes.

An angry retort came to her lips, her usual reaction to the hated name; but this time it died before she had a chance to say it. "Miss Biggity" sounded different to her as George said it, gently and playfully—not scornfully, as Willie did, and the rest of the Negroes at Uphill Farm. George was talking on, leaning toward her with his foot on the carriage wheel.

52

"Your hair looks like a crown, braided and coiled on top of your head. It's mighty pretty that way."

"Cooler, and it won't blow," she replied briefly, still shy with him.

"Mighty pretty," he repeated. "Remember, I'm coming to see you when you get back, and then we'll really get acquainted."

"It'll be a week," she reminded him, and suddenly a week seemed a long time.

"We must go, Jonas," the mistress called. "We've a long day's ride ahead, and it's going to be hot."

Jonas cracked the whip over the horses, and the carriage rolled onto the highroad. Mr. Harry and George mounted their horses again, and the last thing Josephine Charlotte saw as she looked back was the two men sitting there waving them out of sight as they rounded the first curve on the way to Baltimore.

The coolness of early morning blew away on the dawn wind, and before ten o'clock Josephine Charlotte was dripping hot under the clear blue sky. When Jonas stopped at a shady watering trough to water the horses and rest them for a few minutes, the mistress looked at her hot face and insisted she sit with them inside the carriage where she would be shaded from the sun.

The stage from Baltimore north to Pennsylvania passed them, and Mistress Elizabeth amused them with the story of the great stage robbery of a few years before. Master Robert had been sheriff at the time, and had never ceased talking about it.

"I wish something like that would happen on this

trip," Miss Sarah sighed wistfully. "I'd like something really exciting!"

"Just going to Baltimore is exciting enough for me," Josephine said.

Mistress Elizabeth nodded, loosened her dress at the throat and fanned herself. "Jonas," she put her head out of the window and called to him, "remember we're going to stop at the Winstons' place at noon."

"It's not more than five miles down the road, Mistress," he called back. "It's a mite hot. The horses need a rest."

They all needed a rest by the time Jonas turned the sweating horses off the highroad into the long drive that led to the Winstons' big house. They drew up at the horseblock, and a houseboy came out to meet them. He knew the mistress at once and ran back in to announce the visitors. In a moment Mistress Mary Winston bustled out onto the veranda to greet them. They were urged to come in and were shown up to a guest chamber to rest before dinner.

Mistress sank onto the bed with a sigh of relief. Josephine poured cool water into the basin, wrung out a cloth and laid it on Mistress Elizabeth's hot forehead. She wondered if this trip might be too much for her, with the pregnancy almost eight months advanced.

"My hair makes me so hot!" Sarah complained.

She kept lifting her heavy curls from her neck and finally Josephine Charlotte said,

"Let's pin them up. It will be ever so much cooler."

54

Sarah agreed, so the rest of the time before dinner was spent arranging the soft golden curls in a becoming cluster on top of her head. Jo barely had time to wash her own face before the dinner gong sounded through the house and they went downstairs. Josephine Charlotte ate her meal in the kitchen with the house slaves, who were frankly envious of her trip into the city.

"Oh my," sighed the old mammy who had nursed all of the Winston children for two generations, "and aren't you the lucky one, young as you are and getting the chance to see the big city! Here I am, an old woman, just half a day's journey away and I've never been closer than Perry Hall. At my age I'll never get there, I 'spose."

Josephine Charlotte felt sorry for her and tried to be politely modest about her good fortune, but they kept throwing questions at her so she had to tell them about the wedding and her commission to make the blue velvet pelisse.

"What's going to become of you after the wedding, Josie?" one of the young black girls wanted to know.

All of the sunshine died out of the day for Josephine Charlotte.

"I don't know," she murmured. "Nobody has told me."

But in her ears echoed Willie's whispered reminder of the morning.

"It won't be long now, Josie."

chapter 7

THE MOON WAS shining on Baltimore when the carriage rolled down Fayette Street where Uncle Corbin lived. He was waiting for them, sitting on his wide veranda in the soft summer night, chatting with someone hidden in the shadows. He hurried to the horse block to greet them and help the ladies down. He kissed the mistress lightly on the cheek and swept Sarah up in his arms and held her there with her small feet dangling off the ground. She had been almost asleep with the lulling motion of the carriage in the warm dark, but now she was wide awake and giggling in her uncle's arms.

56

"I'm not a little girl any longer, Uncle Corbin," she protested. "I'm practically a married woman, you know."

Her uncle set her down on her feet, but kept his arm around her.

"So I'm told," he agreed, "but I can't believe it. What goings-on while I turned my back and went to Europe! I left you a little girl, racing around the farm on that big black horse, and I return to find you a bride. Where's Josephine Charlotte? Didn't you bring her?"

"Of course I brought her," Sarah assured him, reaching up to smooth her curls. "I couldn't possibly choose my trousseau without her."

Josephine Charlotte had jumped out of the carriage on the other side and was helping the houseman unload luggage. Now she came around to Uncle Corbin and dropped him a curtsey. She knew him well, for he often came to visit at Uphill Farm.

They walked up onto the veranda, while Jonas drove the tired horses back to the stables. The man in the shadows stood up and came forward.

"Why, William," cried Mistress Elizabeth, "I had no idea we'd find you here. I thought you were traveling!"

"I was," replied the tall gray man, smiling at her, "but I ran into Corbin on my way home, and he insisted that I stop for a visit with him. Then he told me that my cousins from Uphill Farm were coming down to shop, so here I am and here thee is. How delightful!"

Josephine Charlotte had been puzzled when she first saw him. In the dim light he didn't seem at all familiar to her, but now she knew; he was the master's Cousin William, a devout Quaker who lived in Fallston and seldom came to stay at Uphill Farm. She did remember very vividly one of his rare visits. On a summer evening he had strolled out to the slave quarters to see her grandmother, whom he seemed to know well.

He had stood talking to the old slave woman in front of her cabin, with Josephine playing around her skirts. In the years since that time one thing he said had remained clear and sharp in her memory.

"Mark my words, Granny," he had said with a curious urgency in his voice, "it won't come in thy time, and probably not in mine, but it *will come*. Perhaps when thy little Jo, here, is grown up . . ."

His voice had trailed off, and he had patted her curly head and wandered away in the dusk. Josephine Charlotte scarcely remembered seeing Cousin William since that night. She had asked her grandmother what was "going to come," perhaps when she grew up; but Grandmother only answered, "You're too young to understand. Run along to bed."

Now here he was after all those years, searching her face in the moonlight and asking,

"Can this be Granny's Josephine Charlotte? Thee is so grown-up!"

The travelers were so tired that they ate the supper Uncle Corbin's cook had waiting for them and went straight up the winding staircase to bed. The mistress had a room to herself, and the girls shared a room down the hall. Josephine hung up their dresses and went to help the mistress, but Ellie, one of Uncle Corbin's house slaves, had been in to turn down the bed and unpack her luggage.

That night Josephine Charlotte slept on a folded blanket on the floor beside Miss Sarah's bed. It wasn't as comfortable as her trundle bed at Uphill Farm, but she didn't mind—she didn't mind anything as long as she was in Baltimore. Tomorrow they would go shopping and buy cloth for the wedding gown and look for some beautiful blue velvet and perhaps some ostrich feathers for the hat. She was asleep on her hard bed before the plans were done.

Mistress Elizabeth and Sarah were given breakfast in bed the next morning. Sarah's blue eyes were wide with wonder when Ellie rapped at the door and brought in a tray set with the dantiest of pink and white china and a silver pot of hot chocolate. Josephine Charlotte heaped pillows behind Sarah's back and went down to have her own breakfast in the kitchen with the other slaves. Later she went into the parlor where the family was discussing plans for the day.

"Go downtown shopping today if you like, Sarah," Uncle Corbin was saying as she came in, "but as a special favor to me, don't buy the cloth for your wedding gown. I've a special reason for asking."

"All right," Sarah replied, hesitantly, "but that's the most important thing we have to do this week, you know, Uncle Corbin. We'll need plenty of time to look."

"Look all you want, baby," he said with his big, hearty laugh, "but just don't buy it yet."

Jonas took them downtown in the carriage and waited while they walked up and down busy Baltimore Street and looked in the show windows. Sarah had been in Baltimore before, but to Josephine Charlotte it was all an enchanting dream come true. They went to the biggest shops and looked at all the beautiful materials. Finally they began to shop seriously in Brooks and Thresher's store. A tall woman with bright red hair done in the most elaborate curls waited on them and brought out bolt after bolt of heavy white silk and shimmering satin.

"The very latest for wedding gowns," she told them in her superior manner, holding up a length of it for them to admire. "Woven in England of silk thread imported direct from the Orient."

"Oh," said Sarah, "isn't it *beautiful*? Mama, I do wish we could buy it *now*. Why do you suppose Uncle Corbin wants me to wait?"

Mistress Elizabeth smiled. "Nobody in this world but Corbin knows why he wants you to wait; but knowing your uncle, I suggest you do as he says."

"All right," Sarah agreed reluctantly, "but we can buy the velvet for my pelisse today, anyhow. We want blue velvet," she informed the saleslady.

Josephine Charlotte stood back as the bolts of soft, sumptuous velvet were laid on the counter, though she could hardly control her urge to reach out and touch it. Finally they saw a deep, rich blue that suited Sarah

60

perfectly.

"There!" she exclaimed. "That's the one I want. What do you think, Mama? How do you like the shade, Jo?"

"Oh dear," complained the mistress in her indecisive manner, "how I wish I knew more about materials. I just don't know, Sarah. I suppose it will have to be whatever you want."

The saleswoman stepped into the situation instantly. "You won't like that," she announced haughtily. "We've had this color in stock for years. It's really quite old-fashioned. Now take this slate blue. It's the very latest for winter; it'll be seen at the best places. The quality is better, too."

"I don't like the color as well," Sarah protested, "but if it's better material, and it's newer . . . Oh, I don't know, either." She turned to look at Josephine. "What do you think, Jo?"

This was Josephine Charlotte's cue. She moved quietly forward to look at the cloth. Her eyes fell on the prices marked on the ends of the bolts. The slate blue was considerably more expensive than the one Sarah liked. She picked it up and held it under Miss Sarah's chin.

"Mmmm," she murmured. "Makes your eyes look washed out. We'll try the other one."

She held up the deep blue velvet and smiled with satisfaction. Mistress Elizabeth smiled, too. Josephine gently steered Sarah to a long pier glass at the end of the counter and said, "See how it deepens the color of your eyes?"

Miss Sarah saw and said firmly to the disappointed clerk,

"We'll take this. She's right, as usual. It's much better with my eyes."

In the meantime, Josephine Charlotte was feeling the texture of the two velvets to make sure that the quality of the first one was quite as good as the second. Mistress Elizabeth paid for the velvet. Josephine Charlotte took the bulky parcel, and they wandered around the store until they found fluffy white ostrich plumes to compliment the deep blue velvet. Jonas was waiting in front with the carriage, so they were back in the big, cool house on Fayette Street in a short time.

Plans were under way for a gala dinner that evening. Some relatives who lived in the city had been invited, and Cousin William was staying on for the festivities. Mistress Elizabeth, quite fatigued, disappeared into her room for a long nap, and Sarah and Josephine Charlotte went upstairs to admire the velvet at leisure. Jo draped its lustrous blue length around Sarah's shoulders and stuck the snowy ostrich plumes in her hair.

"My!" she exclaimed. "You'll be the belle of Harford County in that outfit."

Miss Sarah pirouetted in front of the long mirror and purred with pleasure. "Let's go home and make it right away, Jo," she cried. "I can't wait!"

"You'll have to wait," chuckled Josephine Charlotte. "There's a wedding dress to buy yet, remember?"

'So there is," yawned Sarah. "Well, all right. We'll stay a while longer, but I do wish Uncle Corbin wouldn't be so mysterious about it. I'm going to bed for a while. Why don't you take a nap, too?"

"I'm not tired," Josephine objected. "What a waste of time to sleep while we're in Baltimore! I can sleep at home. Write me a pass. I want to go for a walk."

"It's too hot to walk, and besides you'll get lost," Sarah objected.

But she wrote a pass on a small piece of paper. Josephine tucked it carefully in the bosom of the green dress, waved a hand at Sarah, and slipped out into the hall and down the winding stairs. The house was quiet. The only sounds came from the kitchen where Ellie and Aunt Mollie, the cook, were deep in preparations for the dinner party that evening. Josephine Charlotte tiptoed through the hall lest she be heard and pressed into service. She wanted to be alone to explore Baltimore—to do it all by herself.

Out on the walk, she drew a long breath and walked swiftly away from the house. Few people were on the street at that hour, and the ones she did meet looked curiously at her. She looked with pleasure at the handsome houses set in green lawns and bright gardens. Before she realized it, she had covered many blocks and knew that she was far away from Uncle Corbin's house. All the way she had been watching for landmarks so she could find her way back.

Now suddenly she was aware of a change in the houses she was passing. They were small and quite shabby, with scrubby little lawns, scuffed by the feet of romping children. There were no beautiful gardens around them, and the people she saw were poorly dressed and some of them were Negroes, free Negroes, she assumed. There were a few free Negroes at home, but they were friendly farm people, quite different from these she was seeing now. She couldn't understand the cold hostility in their eyes as they stared at her, until she remembered she was wearing Miss Sarah's green dress with the black silk slippers.

She began to feel uneasy and had almost decided to turn back when she heard the sound of loud voices near by. Her curiosity got the better of her fears, so she hurried on a block or so farther until she came out into an open square where dozens of people were milling about. They were whites except for a little group of Negroes huddled together at one side. In the middle of the square was a high wooden platform, and on it a white man and a tall, well-built Negro were standing.

"He's young and strong, folks," the white man was saying as she arrived. "Just look at those muscles!" He pushed up the sleeve of the Negro's shirt, and the slave obediently flexed his arm, showing the firm muscles rippling under the bronze skin. "He's a great field hand, but smart enough to train for a house servant. What am I bid? Who'll start the bidding at a hundred and fifty?"

Josephine Charlotte stood in unbelieving silence, listening to the bidding for the young slave standing in the hot sun, sweat running down his face. She had come upon a slave market, and for the first time in her life she was witnessing the auctioning off of a human being. The auctioneer rattled on, pushing the bidding up until someone agreed to pay four hundred dollars for the poor creature on the platform, and marched him off to a waiting wagon.

Josephine Charlotte's stomach was churning, and she felt ill; all she wanted was to run from the sweltering square, back along the shaded streets to Uncle Corbin's big, cool house. She whirled to escape from the wretched place when she heard a moan near her and turned in time to see a young Negro woman making a piteous attempt to hang onto the baby in her arms. An elderly colored woman, tears streaming down her own face, took the baby firmly from her and gave her a gentle push.

"Go on, honey chile," she murmured, "I take good care of the babe, and maybe some day . . ." she choked on the words and her voice trailed off as she cradled the black baby against her breast.

The anguished mother stumbled to the platform, dragged by the auctioneer's helper. Josephine turned again to fly from the horrifying sight when she felt a harsh hand on her arm. A white man pulled her away from the crowd, holding her tightly by the elbow.

"And where might you be going?" he demanded insultingly. "You don't belong around here. Must have stole all those fine clothes from your mistress, and now you're running, eh? Well, let me tell you, that won't work. You come to the wrong place, with all your high and mighty airs."

He leered down at her the way Willie did sometimes, making her flesh crawl. Panic almost got the better of her, but she pulled herself together and remembered the pass tucked in her dress. She pulled it out and had the presence of mind to hold it beyond his reach as he read it.

"I don't believe it," he sneered. "That ain't no real pass. How do I know you didn't git somebody to forge it? Come along and be quiet, or it'll be that much the worse for you."

He grabbed her arm so roughly she flinched with the pain and wondered frantically what to do. If she made a fuss, would anybody in this strange, evil place believe her story and accept her pass as valid? The man had begun to pull her along the bare, baked ground, when she became aware of a tall man coming up behind her and heard a familiar voice saying, calmly,

"What is thee doing with this young woman?"

Josephine Charlotte twisted around to look up into Cousin William's strong, quiet face, but she was still speechless with fear.

"It ain't none of your business what I'm doing with her!" the man snapped. "She's a runaway, that's what she is."

He dug his fingers into her arm again and started for the edge of the square. The tall gray man stepped in front of them and said firmly,

"This is very much my business. This girl belongs to my cousin, and I shall return her where she belongs. Let go of her!"

By this time Josephine Charlotte had found her tongue.

66

"Oh, Mr. William," she cried, "I'm not running away. You know I'm not! Miss Sarah wrote a pass for me, and this man wouldn't believe it was real. I was just out walking."

Cousin William smiled at her reassuringly. "Of course thee wasn't running away," he replied. "Miss Sarah told me thee had gone for a walk, and she was worried for fear thee might get lost. We decided I had better follow thee—at a discreet distance, of course. It appears that it was a good decision!"

Her captor gave them both a fierce look and vanished into the crowd. Josephine Charlotte, still shaking from her experience, walked along beside Cousin William on the way back to the house. He listened attentively to her story.

"Thee shouldn't have come down here by thyself, Jo," he said gravely. "There are all too many men just looking for girls like thee to kidnap and sell to the deep south. If I hadn't come along when I did, the chances are it would have happened to thee."

Josephine Charlotte shuddered. "I didn't mean to go to the slave market," she assured him. "I just found it by accident, and when I saw what was going on, I was so upset I meant to leave right away. But then I stopped to watch that poor girl and her baby. I couldn't bear to see her sold, so I started to leave again, but that horrible man grabbed me."

Cousin William nodded and strode along in silence for a few minutes. Then he said gently,

"Even though thee is a slave, Jo, I'm not at all sure thee knows what slavery really means. Thee has been carefully watched over and loved, first by thy wonderful grandmother and then by the mistress and Miss Sarah. But believe me, dear child, thee should not be *owned*. No human being should ever be *owned* by another!"

"I know," Josephine murmured. "I'm beginning to know it all too well."

She wondered if she should tell him about Willie. The scene at the slave market had kindled her fears into flaming terror. No, she wouldn't tell him now. She still shrank instinctively from sharing this with anyone else, even Cousin William. Perhaps later it would be necessary to ask his help, but now she wanted to manage it alone if she could.

She looked up at the kindly man, and the words he had spoken to her grandmother long ago echoed again in her ears: ". . . it *will come*. Perhaps when thy little Jo, here, is grown up. . . ."

On the impulse she repeated them to him and asked,

"Mr. William, what did you mean? When I asked Grandmother, she said I was too young to know."

Cousin William walked along for some time before he answered her, and then he said, slowly, "Josephine Charlotte, I just told thee that no human being should be owned by another, didn't I?" She nodded, and he went on. "When I said to thy grandmother, 'it will come,' I was referring to the time when no human being in this country will ever again be owned by another. I meant some time slavery will vanish from this land, and all of us, white and black, will live to-

68

gether as free men. It will come. It *must* come!"

Josephine Charlotte stood still on the sidewalk and raised her great dark eyes to his gray ones. "How?" she demanded. "How can it come when there are beasts in the world like the ones I saw today?"

Now they were at Uncle Corbin's gate and Sarah was running across the lawn toward them. Cousin William put his hand on the latch and said softly,

"It will come because there are also people in the world like Sarah. Mark my words, Jo, it will come, and it will come while thee lives!"

chapter 8

"Y OU WERE GONE so long, Jo!" cried Sarah, rushing up to them. "Where in the world have you been?"

Cousin William answered to give Jo time to compose herself.

"I followed her to the slave market," he said calmly. "She was having a bad time with a reprobate who was about to make off with her just about the time I arrived."

"Oh, no!" Sarah exclaimed.

She whirled to Josephine Charlotte, "Why did you ever go to such a place? I can't imagine! Are you all right?"

Watching her mistress exploding like a firecracker served to release Josephine's pent-up feelings, and suddenly she found herself laughing hysterically. Finally she wiped her eyes and explained,

"I didn't mean to go to the slave market, Miss Sarah; I was just walking down this street and I heard such a racket that I went to see what it was all about, and there I was at the slave market. It's a *dreadful* place. I hated it. That's all there was to it."

"Oh no, that isn't all there was to it," Sarah insisted, her blue eyes darting from Jo to Cousin William and back again. "You know very well something happened. Cousin William said so, and I want to know about it."

Once more the Quaker intervened. "All in good time, Sarah," he said. "Ask her about it later when she has had time to calm herself a bit. Now isn't it time for all of us to make ready for thy uncle's dinner party?"

He ruffled her blonde curls and walked off toward the house. Miss Sarah evidently decided to take his advice, for she changed the subject as she and Josephine went up to their room.

"How about the pink muslin tonight, Jo?" she asked, backing up to have her dark blue cotton dress unbuttoned.

"That would be nice," Josephine Charlotte approved.

She laid out the fluffy petticoats for it and the matching pink slippers and the ribbon sash. Then she found the hairbrush and began to brush the shining

71

hair. Mechanically she shaped the curls around her finger and piled them high on top of Miss Sarah's head.

"Beautiful!" she murmured absently, still seeing in her mind the agonized face of the mother in the slave market. Miss Sarah seemed to sense her preoccupation but had the good judgment not to press the matter. Instead she chattered on about the dinner party, while Josephine Charlotte fastened the petticoats and slipped the pink muslin carefully over her head.

"I feel sure Uncle Corbin intends to do something about my wedding gown tonight, Jo," she said. "I can't imagine why he's so mysterious about it, though."

Josephine Charlotte couldn't imagine either. She tore her mind away from the distress of the afternoon and washed her face and combed her own hair. When the sound of the dinner chimes filled the house, they went downstairs, Sarah to the long, elegant dining room, already filling with guests, and Josephine to the kitchen to have her dinner with the house servants.

"Master sure must set great store by your Miss Sarah," said Ellie, the maid. "Have you heard why he's giving this dinner party tonight?"

"Not really," Josephine Charlotte answered. "I supposed it was because she's being married."

"Oh, that's only the half of it, dearie," Ellie replied, while everyone else at the kitchen table stopped to listen. "Master Corbin brought some cloth back from his trip to Europe; you just ought to see it. It's fitten for a queen. There's yards an' yards of it, white satin, shiny as ice, and lace to trim it at least a foot wide."

She stopped talking, and Jo waited impatiently for her to go on, while Ellie simply sat and stared dreamily into space.

"We saw it with our own eyes when Master was un-packing his trunk and we was helpin' him," Tillie took up the story. "Ellie got up nerve to ask him what it was for, him bein' a bachelor an' all, an' he said it was for a weddin' dress for his first niece as got married. It was to be a present for her. Must have cost him a fortune, it's that pretty."

A bell tinkled in the dining room, and Aunt Mollie got heavily to her feet.

"Like as not they're ready for pie," she said, bustling into the pantry. "Josie, you go into the dining room an' fetch the dishes out. It'll give you a chance to see what's goin' on in there."

Josephine Charlotte went gratefully and began to clear the dinner plates away. Mistress Elizabeth was playing hostess for the evening, sitting opposite Uncle Corbin at the head of the table. Miss Sarah sat next to her uncle, chatting with people that Josephine had never seen before. At that moment Uncle Corbin stood up and prepared to make a speech, while Josephine slowed up as much as she dared.

"During my recent trip abroad," he began, clearing his throat and taking a sip of water, "I found many beautiful things in the shops, especially things that a daughter would love, if I had one. I steeled myself against the temptation to buy most of them, but one thing I decided to bring back for the first of my many nieces who married after my return."

He paused and looked at Miss Sarah, sitting motionless in her pink muslin dress. "Sarah, the first news to greet me when I came back to Maryland was of your engagement and approaching marriage. Stand up, my dear, and receive your present."

Sarah arose, blushing and smiling, and Uncle Corbin clapped his hands. Like magic his houseboy appeared carrying a large package, beautifully wrapped in white tissue and tied with a wide satin ribbon. He presented it to the bride with a deep bow and flourish. She sat down, had the paper off in an instant, and began to unfold yards and yards of shimmering, creamy white satin. Josephine Charlotte had given up all pretense of clearing the table and stood in back of the Mistress' chair, watching.

"Oh, Mama, isn't it *beautiful?*" Sarah cried. "Just look at it. There's enough for a gorgeous wedding gown. Jo, come here and look! Oh, and there's lace, too. Did you ever see such *lovely* lace?"

She held it up against her, unaware for the moment of anyone except her mother and Josephine Charlotte. Then suddenly she dropped it on the table, and flung herself into Uncle Corbin's arms, as he stood smiling at her.

Later that evening when the guests were all gone and Mistress Elizabeth had retired, quite exhausted with the events of the day, Sarah and Josephine slipped into her room where she lay in the big four-poster, propped up with pillows, and spread the shining white satin around her so that they could all admire it again. Sarah and her mother stroked it with disbelief, as if they could hardly believe it was real.

"It's so lovely," the mistress said. "We could never have afforded anything of half such quality, Sarah. Just feel how heavy it is, Jo."

Josephine Charlotte took a fold between her slender fingers and nodded. "I know," she agreed, "and there's so much of it that it can be made any style Miss Sarah chooses. Miss Minnie will certainly enjoy working on this satin."

Sarah sighed regretfully. "You know, Jo," she said. "I wish *you* were going to make it yourself, instead of Miss Minnie."

"Oh no," Josephine protested, "I wouldn't attempt anything like this. I think I can make the blue velvet pelisse all right, with her help, but I'd never dare cut into satin like this!"

"Jo's right," Mistress Elizabeth nodded, appreciating Jo's good judgment. "She sews beautifully, but she's not had the experience for this. Give her time and I believe she will be able to do anything; but for this we'll have Miss Minnie. Do remind me tomorrow, we shall have to go and see her and make all the arrangements. Now you girls run along to bed. I need my rest."

Miss Sarah was asleep almost as soon as her head touched the pillow, but Jo lay awake, still shaky from her fright in the slave market, her mind full of dark thoughts and fears that she could not drive away. She heard Uncle Corbin and Cousin William come up to

bed and stand talking in the corridor. Their discussion came to her clearly through the door, evidently the continuation of one begun downstairs.

"Now, now, William," Uncle Corbin's deep voice came to her in a subdued roar. "I think you're unduly alarmed. Granted the child had an unfortunate experience this afternoon, and granted some slaveholders abuse their privileges, still I believe you Quakers take an unrealistic attitude toward the Negroes. They aren't all mistreated and they aren't all unhappy, that I know. I don't know a single slave owner in our family who isn't confounded considerate of them."

"I don't care how considerate thee, or anybody else in the family, is of thy slaves, the whole philosophy of slavery is wrong," Cousin William responded, his voice rising. "And some day it's going to blow wide open. No human being has any business owning another human being, no matter what color. Imagine a talented, intelligent, beautiful young girl like Josephine Charlotte being *owned*. Revolting!"

"Well, I admit that she is 'somethin' special,' as her granny used to say," answered Uncle Corbin, a note of apology creeping into his voice. "But for one like her, there are a million who are quite inadequate, quite in need of custody. Cousin, I'm afraid you're a visionary and an idealist, and don't really know what you're talking about."

"Thee is right about Josephine Charlotte," said Cousin William, softly. "In fact, she's so special that if I had the money I'd buy her from Robert tomorrow and set her free. Goodnight, Cousin Corbin. I'm afraid thee and I will never see eye to eye on this issue."

Josephine Charlotte heard two bedroom doors close, and she turned over with her face in the blanket and cried herself to sleep.

chapter 9

THE NEXT TWO DAYS were a little boring for Josephine Charlotte. Miss Sarah was invited out for
tea both afternoons and to an evening party, while Jo
stayed in the house with nothing much to do except
help Aunt Mollie in the kitchen and chat with Ellie.
They soon exhausted what little they had in common,
and after that Josephine amused herself by sketching a
variety of designs for the wedding gown. It was fun to
pretend that she *was* going to make it. After her terrifying experience the first day of their visit, she was
afraid to go walking, so she was glad when Mistress
Elizabeth announced they would return to Uphill

Farm a day earlier than planned.

"There are so many things to do at home before the wedding," she explained to the girls, as though she were afraid they would be disappointed. Josephine Charlotte suspected part of the reason was her growing fatigue.

"It's so hot, too," she sighed, fanning herself. "I never could stand heat very well. I guess I should have stayed at home and sent you girls alone with Jonas."

Jo took the fan and kept the air stirring over her flushed face, well aware that the mistress was dreading the long ride home and the endless conversation with Miss Minnie, who was exceedingly chatty. Sarah was glad to go.

"We've had a lovely time," she said, "but now it's time to go home and do things. Do you realize there are only three weeks left before I'm married?"

Josephine Charlotte realized it all too well. The excitement of the trip and the visit had pushed from her mind the ominous remark Willie had made before their departure, but now it came back. She remembered the triumphant smirk on his face when he said,

"Master Robert gonna sell us to pay for Miss Sarah's weddin'."

So it was in a mood of deep depression that she said farewell to Cousin William early the next morning as he mounted his tall dapple-gray mare to set out for Fallston, promising to arrive at Uphill Farm in plenty of time for the wedding. She thought she was concealing her unhappiness quite well until he leaned down from his horse and spoke to her softly.

"Josephine Charlotte, what is the matter with thee? I can see that thee is greatly troubled."

"I am," she whispered, "but I can't tell you now. Perhaps when you come to Uphill Farm."

He nodded and walked his horse down the drive. She watched him go sadly, wondering if she would ever see him again, this kind, gentle Quaker who seemed to be the only one she could turn to for help. Yet the small Quaker village where he lived might as well have been a thousand miles away. The carriage was brought to the horse block, and Uncle Corbin helped the mistress in and chatted gaily with Sarah.

"I'll be there, don't you fret," he assured her. "I wouldn't be likely to miss such an event in the family. I'll come early and stay late, and you tell Miss Minnie to do her best with that wedding gown."

Josephine Charlotte climbed up beside Jonas. It reminded her of their leaving Uphill Farm almost a week before and of her thrill when George so unexpectedly appeared at the gate to see them off. Suddenly her melancholy vanished like the morning mist. George would be waiting for her, and she would look up into that bright brown gaze again.

Master Robert couldn't be planning to take her away from Miss Sarah before the wedding—he could never do such a thing to them, and Willie couldn't hurt her if George was there to intervene. She smiled at Jonas and settled into her seat for the long day, calling good-bye to Uncle Corbin and all of his servants who had come out to see them off.

They stopped briefly on Jones Street to pick up Miss

Minnie and her luggage, and then they were off at a steady trot for Harford County. All morning long, with the sun climbing higher and breathing more heat upon them every mile, they journeyed toward Uphill Farm, Miss Minnie chatting happily all the way. This time they stopped for dinner and rest at another cousin's farm, and when they resumed their travels in the middle of the afternoon, Miss Minnie resumed her chatter, too; Josephine Charlotte could hear its clicking, rhythmic cadence, although she couldn't make out the words. Occasionally it would be punctuated by a rejoinder in Mistress Elizabeth's gentle voice or Sarah's gay laughter. She could picture how weary the mistress must be with the long ride and the tedious prattle.

It was an uneventful trip, with only a few carriages on the road and even fewer horsemen. The stagecoach rumbled by on its way up to Philadelphia, and Josephine remembered Sarah's half-joking, half-serious wish that something exciting like a stagecoach robbery might happen to them. Misty blue twilight was settling over the hills now, and the great trees that covered them cast dark shadows across the road. Josephine Charlotte stared apprehensively into the depths of the forest and felt the smothering black mood of the morning enveloping her again. She let her mind dwell at last upon the thing she had pushed away from her for so many days.

If she ran away, it would have to be at night, when the forests were dark and forbidding. The pleasant, sunny roads with their occasional travelers could not be for a fugitive slave. In the daytime she would have to hide, sleeping in the deepest part of the wood, seeking the protective coloration of the ferns and grasses and underbrush. At night she would creep through the forest as silently and furtively as the wild things that dwelt there, the timid, soft-eyed deer and the noiseless rabbits and the scurrying field mice. Like a shadow without substance she would move night after night through the infinity of trees toward her destination, the Susquehanna River, where she would find an old black man called Richard Harris, who would row her across the river on her way to safety.

Her gloomy meditation was interrupted by Jonas' clearing his throat and looking uneasily over his shoulder into the darkness of the woods.

"Kind of scary at night, ain't it?" he asked, flicking his horses with the whip. They quickened their pace, and Jonas sighed and went on talking.

"Jest afore we left home," he said, "a man stopped by an' tol' us about huntin' wolves over on Winter's Run. Shot one hisself. I don' reckon they'd come out on the road a summer night like this, though, jest in the winter when they're hungry, like as not."

Josephine Charlotte thought his remark lacked conviction; it sounded more like a question. He hunched his shoulders and waved his whip over the team again.

"Jonas, are there *bears* in the woods?" She blurted out the question involuntarily, clenching her hands in her lap and moving closer to him on the seat.

"Oh sure," he nodded, lapsing into reminiscence, comforted somehow by the sound of his own voice.

82

"Lots of bears in the woods. Didn' you never see 'em winter mornin's, comin' out to look for somepin' to eat around the pastures? Why, when I was a little feller, I even seen 'em come clean up to the kitchen door, snufflin' round for food."

They both fell silent, and there was no sound on the road but the beat of the horses' feet in perfect rhythm, carrying them home. Even Miss Minnie's chatter had ceased, and Josephine Charlotte suspected that everyone inside the carriage had fallen asleep. She shut her own eyes to hide the awesome dark of the forest and close her mind to what lay within it. She must have slept, for the next thing she knew the horses were turning briskly into the drive at Uphill Farm, trotting toward their oats in the stable. Candles were gleaming in the windows of the big house; the three small brothers came racing out, shouting to their mother, and the rest of the family followed. Master Robert was there to lift his tired wife down from the carriage and give Miss Minnie a hand. Josephine Charlotte climbed down from the high seat, foggy with sleep, and there beside the wheel stood Willie, waiting for her.

"Back from the big city, Miss Biggity," he greeted her, reaching out for her with his big hands.

She darted around to the other side of the carriage to carry the precious packages in, hoping to elude him until the morning, but he followed her up the winding stairs, carrying Miss Sarah's luggage. He set the valises down in their room, and on his way out the door he turned and whispered loudly to her,

"Master wants to see you first thing in the mornin'. It's just like I said. He done tol' me so tonight; he goin' to see that we get married, but I got it all planned better. You meet me out in the pasture, t'other side of the hill. We'll git on a horse an' ride to the preacher an' git married ourselves. It'll be less trouble all 'round. Now mind, you meet me in the mornin', sun-up."

Josephine Charlotte's mind, after the first numbing paralysis, worked with lightning speed. She shut the door slowly and said softly, through the crack,

"All right, Willie. I won't fight you any more. I'll see you in the morning."

She stood with her back to the door, leaning against it for support, feeling drained of all life. It had come so soon, much sooner than she had dreamed. Now it seemed that Willie had been telling the truth when he said the master intended to sell them to pay for the wedding. With her doubts fading, she regretted that she had shrunk from discussing it with anybody, especially Cousin William. Now it was too late. She should have asked him what to do when she talked with him in Baltimore, instead of waiting until he was far away in Fallston. Now there was no one. She couldn't possibly ask Miss Sarah, not under the circumstances. For it did seem true. The tobacco was bad, and the wedding would be expensive.

She heard Mistress Elizabeth's weary steps on the stairs, and Miss Minnie with her, chattering again. The children were running up to their rooms, and in a few minutes Sarah and the other girls came along and stopped outside the door to talk. Josephine Charlotte thought she would die if they came in; but the talk went on in the hall, and she moved away from the door and automatically turned Sarah's bed down for the night and got out her nightdress and slippers. She lit the candles on the bureau and poured water into the washbowl. All of these familiar things she did without thinking, and she was barely aware of the conversation in the hall until she heard her name.

"Jo will start on the blue velvet tomorrow," said Sarah. "She has about three weeks until the wedding. I don't know how she'll ever get it done."

"Don't worry about Jo," Ellen reassured her. "You know how fast she is. It's Miss Minnie I'd worry about if I were you. She's good, but she's slow."

"I know," Sarah yawned, "but I guess it will all work out. Now I've got to go to bed. I'm so tired."

Mary Ann and Ellen went on down the hall, and Sarah opened the door and came in, fortunately much too sleepy to talk. Josephine helped her out of her dress, and in a minute had bathed her face, braided her hair and had her ready to go to sleep in the high bed.

"Aren't you coming to bed, Jo?" she asked, because the trundle bed wasn't pulled out yet.

"By and by," Josephine Charlotte answered. "I'll snuff the candles so you can go to sleep. I can see well enough by the light of the moon."

She moved noiselessly about the room, setting it to

rights, hanging up the clothes, emptying the wash-bowl. She listened for the sound of regular breathing to tell her when Miss Sarah was asleep. While she waited, she sat down by the window in the moon-light. Her mind was a blank; what she had to do she would do with only instinct to guide her. At last she heard the soft breathing grow measured and slow. She rose from the window and went to the wardrobe to find her oldest brown calico dress and the heavy leather shoes she wore in the cold weather or when walking in the woods. She put on the dress and but-toned it with shaking fingers. With her shoes in her hand she went without a sound to the bed where Sarah lay sleeping.

"Good-bye, my little missy," she whispered, quite dry-eyed; this was no time for tears. She bent to put her lips against the shining hair in a fleeting kiss and was gone from the room, lost in the shadows of the silent house. She must find a little food; there wasn't time to gather much, and she couldn't carry it, anyway. In the kitchen there was bread, so she took part of a loaf and a piece of meat and went out into the night.

The moon was so bright she was afraid she might be seen leaving the house, but she hid a few minutes in the shadows of the trees along the drive, and there was no alarm, so she knew that no one was abroad at Uphill Farm. It was safe for her to go on her way. She moved down the curving drive and across the highroad, her face set toward the Susquehanna River where she must search until she found old Richard Harris. She dared not stop to think of what lay ahead of her in the woods, or that she knew nothing, really, of the way to the river. Josephine Charlotte looked back just once at the big house, glimmering white in the moonlight through the trees, and then she took a great breath and plunged into the fearful forest.

chapter 10

GEORGE AWOKE at dawn where he slept in the loft above the kitchen at Mr. Harry's house. He lay still on the straw tick for a few minutes, thinking of the day ahead. This was the day he had been waiting for; the family was returning from Baltimore, and he would be there to welcome Josephine Charlotte home. Mr. Harry would be going over on his sleek bay riding horse to see Miss Sarah, of course. It would be a joyful homecoming, and George stretched and smiled with pleasure at the thought. The sun glinted through the cracks in the walls, and it reminded him of how beautifully it had shone on Jo's glowing bronze face and arms the morning she had left for the city. It had seemed a long week; but now it was over, and he would see her again. For the first time they would be alone together and could really talk.

He got up and put on his old work trousers and shirt and went down to the well to wash in a bucket of cold water. He felt wonderful, with the cool morning wind blowing against him. Then just as he was about to go into the kitchen to see what Aunt Melissy had for breakfast, he heard a horse on the road, still out of sight around the curve. It was coming fast, its feet thudding on the dry dirt; and as it came into sight, George was startled to see Master Robert's Jonas riding at full gallop on one of Uphill Farm's fast horses.

Jonas whirled into the yard and pulled his horse to a stop. He leaped down and ran to George, his black face strained and anxious.

"George, you come quick. Git Mr. Harry and git on yo' horses and come right away," he cried. "Things is in an awful state. Miss Sarah's cryin', the mistus is wringin' her hands, and Josephine Charlotte's *gone*."

"Jo's *gone?*" cried George. "What do you mean she's gone? And what are you doing home? You were coming home today. You just calm down and tell me what's goin' on."

"Don' ask no questions!" Jonas implored. "Git up on yo' horse an' come."

But he managed to quiet himself enough to explain a little.

"We come home last night," he said. "Mistus wasn't feelin' good so we come a day early. Everybody was tired an' went straight to bed. Miss Sarah went to sleep right smart, but Josie was still up. Miss Sarah remembers she asked her wasn't she comin' to bed, and Josie said pretty soon. This mornin' Miss Sarah done woke up early. Josie's bed wa'n't even slept in, an' she's *gone*. Miss Sarah woke everybody up an' the whole fambly an' all the colored folks been lookin' for her, an' she's *gone*, I tell you. Miss Sarah said I was to ride for you and Mr. Harry fast as I could, so git on a horse an' come!"

Without another word George started for the house and met Mr. Harry coming out. He explained briefly what had happened and threw the harness on the horses. In a few minutes the three men were galloping down the road to Uphill Farm. The whole family was assembled on the veranda when they turned their horses into the long drive. Jonas was right; Miss Sarah was crying, and the mistress was literally wringing her hands. Master Robert was pacing back and forth, and they arrived in time to hear Sarah moaning.

"But Papa, she wouldn't run away. Whatever would make Jo run away? I know something dreadful has happened to her!"

Master Robert shrugged his shoulders and threw up his hands in complete bafflement, but Mary Ann spoke up pertly.

"Of course she'd run away, Sarah, if she got a good chance. I've told you for ages you've ruined her— absolutely ruined her. Now you see I was right. You just can't spoil darkies like that without trouble."

Sarah didn't honor her remark with a reply. She saw

Mr. Harry and George coming and flew to meet them, tears streaking her cheeks. Harry gathered her into his arms, disregarding the presence of the family, and George stood back and waited while Sarah sobbed out her story. Finally, she lifted her head from his shoulder and accepted his handkerchief to wipe her eyes. She turned to George, wailing.

"What are we going to do, George? What could have happened?"

George shook his head, feeling as helpless as she did. When he had said good-bye to Josephine Charlotte a week before, he believed she felt sorry to leave him and would be happy to see him again. Now she was gone, and he had to confess utter perplexity. He stood shaking his head, wishing that Miss Sarah would stop looking at him so expectantly.

Mistress Elizabeth leaned back limply in a basket chair, watching him anxiously. Suddenly she sat up straight and said to her husband,

"Robert, I think we should send for Cousin William. I just remembered when he was with us in Baltimore he spent considerable time with Jo. He found her and brought her back the day she had such a bad experience at the slave market. I told you about that. Maybe he would know what to do. He might even have some idea of what made her run away."

Sarah ran to her mother and knelt beside her.

"Mama," she implored, the tears starting to flow again, "don't *you* say she ran away, too. I can't bear it if you think so. I know she didn't. I *know*, but even if she did, there was some reason we don't know about.

There was some reason, I tell you."

The mistress stroked her hair and said gently, "I know you want to believe that, daughter, and I do, too; but we have to find out why she disappeared if we're ever to find her. I believe Cousin William would know; Quakers help so many slaves—" she faltered and then went on, "to go away."

Master Robert nodded and said, "I believe you're right, Elizabeth. Let's have William here. Confounded inconsiderate of her to upset Sarah like this just before the wedding, and all!"

George stepped forward. "I'll go, sir," he offered. "Please let me go."

He thought that anything would be better than standing here with nothing to do, feeling miserable and helpless.

"Oh please, Papa, do let George go," Sarah pleaded. "He's such a good rider. Let him ride Midnight."

Master Robert gave his consent and ordered Willie, who had been standing silently on the fringe of the group, to bring Midnight in from the pasture and saddle him.

"He's the fastest horse in the stable," he said. "Take good care of him, George, but ride as fast as you can."

George started out after Willie, but Mistress Elizabeth called to him.

"You haven't had breakfast, George, have you? Stop in the kitchen and ask Aunt Mattie for something to eat. It's quite a way over to Fallston."

"Thank you, Mistress," George replied politely, "but I don't feel hungry right now. I'll eat when I come back."

Eating was the last thing he wanted to do at the moment. His mind was in turmoil and all he could think of was Josephine Charlotte, gone all night in the woods, easy prey for animals, and worse yet, men. She must be in the woods; if she were on the open road, she would have been found and brought back by this time. But, as Miss Sarah said, "Why?" He found Willie saddling Midnight beside the stable.

"Where you 'spose Josie go?" Willie asked him.

George glanced at him carelessly, and then looked again, more closely. Willie's round, fat face was unusually solemn, and George thought suddenly that it was a queer, pasty color. He remembered the afternoon that he had first met Josephine Charlotte at Uphill Farm and Willie had come out of the house, jealous and furious because she was talking to him.

"What do you know about Josephine, Willie?" George demanded. "Don' know nothin'," Willie replied sullenly, his small black eyes regarding him warily. "Why should I know 'bout her?"

"You're the only one who can answer that," George shot back, swinging onto Midnight's back and cantering off to the house.

Master Robert gave him directions to Cousin William's house in Fallston. George knew where the town was, for he had lived not far from there with his first master, so the route was familiar to him. He was eager to be gone, so he cut the farewells as short as he could and set Midnight's feet on the road in an easy lope. He knew well that a breakneck gallop would defeat his purpose.

Midnight traveled steadily, almost as though he knew how much was expected of him. George didn't offer him a rest, and the horse didn't ask for one, even though the sun was brutally hot and lather began to foam out from under the saddle onto his gleaming back. When they came to a woodland shortcut to Fallston that George remembered well, he turned the horse off the road into the cool shade. He slid out of the saddle and walked Midnight slowly up and down the trail for a while before he let him drink from the clear little brook that meandered beside them.

After Midnight had a small drink, not nearly enough to satisfy his thirst, George knelt and cupped the cold spring water into his hands and drank before he started on again. This time he kept the horse at a brisk walk, even though the rest and drink had revived him so he strained to run. Now George had time to look into the depths of the forest as they passed along its aisles, constantly on the alert for the flutter of a calico skirt. He just might find her hiding there, sleeping in the heat of the day, although instinct told him he wouldn't.

He tried not to think why she had gone away, there wasn't any answer he could give. Sarah was so sure that Josephine Charlotte would never have run away from them of her own volition, that something dreadful must have induced her to leave Uphill Farm. George, in spite of the emotion that welled up in him every time he thought of her, found himself uncertain. He knew now that he had fallen in love with her the first time he saw her, that hot afternoon, wearing the cool green dress and looking so beautiful; but that was quite a different matter from knowing her well enough to predict her behavior under stress. Sarah was the one who knew.

The forest began to lighten, its floor dappled with sunlight, and George could see open sky ahead. Midnight moved out into a grassy meadow, and before them the old Quaker burying ground lay at peace under the summer sky, the ancient Meeting House brooding over it. He had been told that Cousin William lived in a small stone cottage close at hand, and there it was, old and gray and slumbrous in the morning heat. George hoped that its owner wasn't drowsing, he was so anxious to be on his way back to Uphill Farm.

Cousin William was working among his flowers in the dooryard when George pulled Midnight to a stop in front of the house. He straightened up and watched the tall young Negro dismounting.

"Thee is welcome," he assured George, holding the gate open for him. "What is thy errand this hot day?"

"Your cousin, Master Robert, sent me to bring you back to Uphill Farm just as fast as possible. You're *needed* there. Will you come?" George implored.

"What's the trouble at my cousin's? Is someone ill?" Cousin William cried. "Of course I will come, but thee must tell me what has happened. Robert would never send for me unless it was serious."

He was walking rapidly toward the small stable as he talked, and George followed him.

"It's none of the family, sir," he explained. "It's Josephine Charlotte; she's missing. She disappeared sometime in the night after the family came back from Baltimore, because this morning when Miss Sarah awoke she was gone. Things are in a bad way over there, and I was sent for you."

"Josephine is gone!" Cousin William exclaimed incredulously. "Why, only yesterday before we parted she said she wanted to talk to me when I came to Uphill Farm for the wedding. This couldn't have been in her mind then. Something must have happened to her; something must have frightened her so badly that she ran away, or somebody took her off. That's a possibility, you know."

He had become so agitated that he stood looking at his two horses, unable to choose. George stepped forward.

"Which one do you want to ride, sir?" he asked quietly. "I'll saddle it."

"The chestnut," replied the tall gray man, regaining his composure. "She's the faster."

George had the harness on her in a moment, and Cousin William rode off beside him without a backward glance at his house. They retraced the path that George had taken, both silent until they were well into the forest; and then Cousin William seemed to remember he had never seen George before.

"Who is thee?" he asked. "I thought I knew all of the Negroes on my cousin's place, but I cannot place thee, somehow. Does thee belong at Uphill Farm?"

96

"No," George told him, pulling Midnight down to match the slower pace of the chestnut. "My name is George, and I belong to Mr. Harry. I haven't been there long."

"Oh, then thee doesn't know Josephine Charlotte very well," Cousin William commented, looking at him keenly. "But thee seems much distressed."

George hesitated before he answered, guiding Midnight carefully around a fallen log.

"It is true that I don't know her very well," he said. "But that doesn't make any difference about my feelings now that she's lost. It just means that I don't know what she would be apt to do if something went wrong. Do you see what I mean?"

Cousin William drew abreast of George and gazed intently at the handsome face. He raised his eyes to look into the intense brown ones that Josephine Charlotte had found so compelling and then, in spite of his anxiety, he smiled.

"George, I do believe thee is in love!"

Momentarily the pain cleared from George's face and he smiled back.

"I do believe I am, too, sir!" he said.

"How does Josephine feel about it?" Cousin William wanted to know. "Is she in love with thee?"

"I don't know," George answered. "I thought she had, well, taken a fancy to me when they left for the city, but we didn't have time to find out. We didn't have time," he repeated forlornly. "I have to find her. You can see why I *have* to find her."

97

He dug his heels into Midnight's flanks, and the horse leaped out of the woods trail and fled down the road toward Uphill Farm, Cousin William on his chestnut, pounding along behind.

chapter 11

COUSIN WILLIAM took charge as soon as they arrived, and he heard the story all over again from Sarah. The family watched in amazement as the gentle Quaker demeanor slipped from him and he ordered people crisply about.

"First of all, Robert," he said, "Elizabeth must be put to bed. This commotion is bad for her in her condition. Mary Ann and Ellen will see to it. Go on, girls, take thy mother upstairs."

He waited until Mistress Elizabeth was led meekly away and then turned again to the master.

"Now, Robert," he said to his cousin, who was

quite unused to taking orders, "the rest of us will sit down and consider this situation as calmly as possible. Now that Elizabeth is gone, we can discuss it more frankly. I didn't wish to upset her further."

"Oh, then you do think it's bad!" cried Sarah.

Harry drew her down beside him on a settee, keeping his arm firmly around her. Cousin William turned his eyes to her and regarded her reflectively for a moment. When he answered, his voice was grave.

"Yes, Sarah," he said, "I think it's bad."

In a moment he went on, breaking the silence that had settled over the group. "I think, Sarah, there are two parts to the puzzle. I can't agree with thee that Jo was taken away forcibly. Since hearing all the details from thee, I have discarded that theory."

He put up his hand to silence the protest that flew to her lips. "Hear me out," he insisted.

George drew closer to Cousin William's chair, and he noticed Willie slouching at the corner of the veranda, as the Quaker continued.

"I have two reasons for thinking this. First, Josephine Charlotte was greatly troubled about something when she bade me goodbye in Baltimore yesterday; and in the second place, she was not ready to retire when thee did last evening. That was somewhat unusual, was it not, because she must have been greatly fatigued after the long drive from the city?"

Sarah nodded. "Yes, I know she was tired, but she just said, 'pretty soon' when I asked her, so I didn't think any more of it. I must have fallen asleep right away, because I didn't hear a thing after that. But,

Cousin William, I'll never believe she *wanted* to leave, no matter what anybody says!"

The gentle note was back in the Quaker's voice when he spoke again.

"No, no, Sarah!" he exclaimed. "I don't believe she wanted to leave, either. I know that Jo loved thee very dearly. Does thee suppose I would be trying to find her if I didn't know that?"

George cringed at the use of the past tense of "love," and he saw that Sarah caught its significance, too.

"As I said," Cousin William proceeded, "something was troubling her when I left Corbin's, and she half promised to tell me about it when I came to the wedding in a few weeks. I believe something happened last night to frighten her so badly that she was induced to run away as a last resort. Now, if we can just find out what bothered her, and what happened to trigger her flight, we may have a chance to find her. If I am correct in assuming that she left of her own free will, I am pretty sure I know where she—."

He cut off his sentence abruptly and sat down.

"You know where she *what*?" Sarah cried, slipping out of Harry's grasp and running to stand in front of him.

George thought he saw a minute flash of mischief in the cool glance William flicked at his cousin Robert.

"In the presence of slaveholders, one of whom was once the sheriff of Harford County," he answered solemnly, "I can tell thee no more."

"Oh!" exclaimed Sarah, momentarily at a loss for

words. "They why don't you just go and get her? Why are you waiting?"

"Because I'm not positive I'm right," said Cousin William, thoughtfully. "I would like to know before we set out—might save us a great deal of fruitless chasing about in the woods. If she were taken away by someone, there's no doubt we wouldn't go 'way over . . . there." And once more George detected the little furtive look, sliding in Master Robert's direction.

"Miss Sarah doesn't have any idea why she went away," Cousin William continued, "and I'm sure if she doesn't, no other white person would. George doesn't know anything about it either. Willie, what does thee know?"

He whirled so swiftly that Willie let out a startled grunt and shrank back around the corner. George thought the pasty look he had observed earlier in the morning had taken on a slight tinge of green.

"What does thee know, Willie?" the Quaker repeated softly, moving toward him.

"Don' know nothin', Massa William," Willie declared, sticking his head out cautiously. "Don' know nothin' at all 'bout Josie."

"I had hoped thee would," the Quaker spoke meditatively now, "because we need to get to her quickly if we get to her at all."

He sighed. "I had hoped not to have to tell thee this," he directed his remarks to Sarah, "but I guess I must. The white man who accosted Josephine Charlotte in the slave market in Baltimore was one of a band of kidnappers operating in Harford County. I have seen him before, and he may have seen me, although he didn't reveal it if he recognized me."

"Kidnappers?" cried Sarah. "What do you mean? They steal children, don't they? What has that to do with Josephine Charlotte?"

"No, they don't steal children—not these men," said Cousin William grimly. "They're after bigger game. They steal Negroes and ship them down the coast to the deep South. They deal mostly with free Negroes, whom they sell into slavery again; but no Negro, male or female, free or slave, is safe from them if found in the deep woods alone. Thee has heard of this splendid, brave bunch of men, no doubt, Robert?" he asked his cousin.

George saw the hot flush that ran from Master Robert's neck up into his face.

"I've heard of them," he agreed, uncomfortably. "They must be a scummy lot."

"You mean," whispered Miss Sarah, her face drained of all its color, so that George thought she would faint, " you mean they may have my Jo *now?*"

"God grant they haven't!" said Cousin William, fervently.

In back of him George heard a strange whining sound, like a hurt animal. Willie came shuffling out from his corner, mumbling under his breath.

"Massa William," he muttered, stopping in front of the Quaker, "I done tol' you a lie. I don' know where Josie go, but I know *why* she go."

The whole miserable, fantastic tale spilled out then.

"You see," Willie finished pathetically, the tears

running down his face like a child, "she never marry with me lessen I scare her into it—she be somthin' so special, an' I ain't nothin'. But a funny thing, Massa William, she *believe* me. Yas suh, she done *believe* me, an' her so smart an' all."

For one triumphant moment the crumpled black face smoothed out into a grin and a tiny gleam of satisfaction lighted the small black eyes, but then great sobs shook his hulking frame again.

"I never thought she run away," he moaned. "When George come to live at Massa Harry's, I knowed I hadda do somethin' quick afore she wanted to marry with him. I seen it all startin'. So I jes tol' her las' night to meet me in the mornin,' an' in the mornin' she was gone. I didn' mean to, I tell you. I jes *loved* her! What we gonna do?"

George's hands, clenched into hard fists while Willie talked, opened and dropped to his sides, and the tense lines in his face relaxed. Willie "jes' loved her," and he loved her, too. To crush Willie to the earth wouldn't do Jo any good now. Suddenly he heard himself speaking.

"We'll go and find her, Willie," he said, as though he were talking to a child.

Cousin William looked at George and suddenly a smile of approval lit his face.

"The three of us will go, George," he said.

Master Robert cleared his throat. "Now William," he said, "you and the boys aren't going into those woods alone. I'll be with you, and we'll get all my darkies out there and find Jo in no time. Don't you cry anymore, baby," he said, turning to Sarah. "We'll have her home right off."

"Well, what about me?" demanded Harry. "I'm certainly going too."

Cousin William shook his head and smiled gently, "Thanks to both of thee, but no. This particular job calls for a Quaker and a couple of Negroes, not a whole crew, and certainly no white slaveowners. Thee both stay home and take care of the ladies. We can't go until evening, anyhow, because we'd be too easily detected."

Sarah had finally gotten the full significance of Willie's story.

"*Why* didn't Jo tell me about it?" she demanded. "I could have set her straight in one sentence; or if she didn't believe me, we could have gone to Papa and talked it all out. Willie, do you really know what you've done? Jo may be lost forever. She may be shipped down to Georgia. We may never see her again! Oh, I can't *bear* it!"

"Yas'm Miss Sarah, I does know what I done," Willie mumbled, hanging his head. "But I never meant to, hones' I didn'."

Master Robert regarded Willie with such disgust that George thought it was a good thing for the culprit that Cousin William was there, or Willie's back might well have felt the lash, seldom used at Uphill Farm.

"Knowing what you've done makes very little difference now, Willie," he said. Then he turned to Sarah and went on,

"I agree with you. *Why* didn't she tell us what was worrying her? How could she imagine that I'd sell her to pay for your wedding?"

Sarah sniffed and wiped her nose. "I think I know how it happened, Papa," she said. "She probably heard you talking that night at dinner about how poor the tobacco was. I myself remember distinctly what you said about selling some Negroes before winter. You see? Then came Willie with his silly story, and what would have seemed a joke to her at any other time didn't seem funny at all. She's so sensitive that she couldn't bear to ask even me about it for fear it was true, and would embarrass me, so she just suffered all by herself. Oh, my poor darling! Think how awful for her! Just put yourself in her place! Willie, I could simply strangle you with my own bare hands!"

"Yes'm," said Willie meekly.

Sarah gave him another furious look and stalked upstairs to wash her face and see how her mother was doing.

The hot, heavy afternoon wore on, with the men sitting on the shady veranda, impatient for evening. George was allowed to stay and hear Cousin William tell about the kidnapping ring, but Willie went off to do his chores before suppertime.

No one knew the exact location of the headquarters, Cousin William explained, although they had a fair idea of the general part of the county. It was supposed to be an abandoned cabin in the deep forest over near the bay. Under cover of darkness a ship could anchor there and the stolen Negroes be taken aboard in irons for the terrible voyage down the coast.

"This may be the night we find it," Cousin William said, grimly.

The bell rang for supper. Sarah came down to fix a tray for her mother and say that she, herself, couldn't eat a bite, and she'd simply die if the baby came before the wedding.

George ate in the kitchen with the house servants and kept an eye on the great black clouds piling up in the West, dropping early twilight over the land. He felt as Sarah did about eating; but on the other hand, he was facing a long night in the woods, with who knew what demands on his strength, so he ate heartily of Aunt Mattie's chicken and biscuits and blueberry pie, and felt strangely better.

Cousin William came for him as soon as supper was over, and they found Willie waiting for them with the horses. They had decided to save time by riding as much as they could, even though the trails were narrow through the forest. It was almost dark now, and they walked the horses down the long drive and out onto the road. In just a few minutes they turned off into the deep forest, as the first clap of thunder echoed over the hills and rumbled away in the distance.

chapter 12

THE LIGHTNING flashed and great peals of thunder,
rolling over the sky, died away in the caverns of
the forest. Willie flung himself flat along his horse's
back and hid his face in the long chestnut mane.
Cousin William, leading the way along the shadowy
trail, glanced back and saw him.

"Sit up and watch where thee's going, Willie!" he
commanded sternly.

"Can't, Massa William," moaned Willie, beside
himself with fear. "I so scared. You better believe me,
we never should a started out in this storm. You better
believe we never find Josie a night like this—this a

bad sign."

George crowded his horse up beside Willie's and took hold of the bridle.

"I'll lead him, Mr. William," he said in exasperation. "Where are we heading?"

"Richard Harris' place on the Susquehanna," the Quaker replied briefly. "I expect thee's heard of him, George?"

"I've heard of him," George responded. "He's taken a few folks I know across. You think Josephine Charlotte would go there?"

"Yes, I think he's the only person she'd know about around here to help her. Poor child, if only she had confided in me! I know many Quakers in the neighborhood."

Willie raised his head from the protection of the horse's mane and ducked back again as a blazing flash of lightning illumined the forest.

"Miss Biggity make us all a lot of trouble, she so uppity," he mumbled.

George snorted indignantly. "If I were you, I wouldn't talk about Jo making anybody a lot of trouble," he retorted. "If it hadn't been for you, we'd all be safe where we belong."

Willie subsided, and the riders proceeded in a silence broken only by the swishing of the wind high in the trees and the roar of the thunder.

"The heat's stifling," complained Cousin William, drawing out his kerchief to wipe the sweat from his forehead. "Wouldn't you think the rain would come with all this storm?"

The rain did come with the next mighty crash—a torrential, drenching rain that saturated the men and the forest in moments. Cousin William brought out his kerchief again to mop his streaming face.

"Can't see where we're going," he shouted over the noise of the storm, "but we're better off moving. Friend John Minton's place is on this trail; I'm afraid it's still a long way, though."

George said nothing, just slogged along, pulling Willie's horse with him, but the more violent the storm grew, the tighter the knot in his stomach became. He could think of nothing but Josephine Charlotte alone in the woods.

"This is the second night for her. Could she have reached the Susquehanna yet?" he called out to William.

If only he could know that she was safe from the wild storm in the home of old Richard Harris!

"Not on foot," William called back. "She would have had to hide during the day and start out again this evening. In all this storm and not knowing her way, she couldn't have arrived there yet. Let's just pray that she hasn't strayed from the trail. We'll go to Harris' place if we don't overtake her on the way; and if she isn't there, I know several Quakers in the vicinity who will help us search for her tomorrow."

"We can't wait for tomorrow!" George exclaimed. "I, for one, am going on all night."

"Of course," the Quaker soothed him. "We'll all go on unless the storm gets worse and we can't."

The storm continued in unabated fury, the rain so

heavy and the night so black that Cousin William could scarcely see the trail at all. Several times he had to dismount and search for it on foot, leading his frightened horse. They shivered in the sudden chill that came with the rain. Without the lightning, they would have been lost.

"I must confess I don't really know where we are," said the Quaker in the silence and the darkness that followed a savage crash. "In the daytime, or even on an average night I'm pretty familiar with this part of the forest, but this is the worst I've ever seen."

Willie was quick to see his chance.

"Massa William," he implored, "let's go back home and wait 'til daylight. The good Lord done send all this thunder an' lightnin' to warn us to git back. We can' do Josie no good iffen we git lost, too, or maybe killed."

"If we keep to the trail, we won't get lost," George declared. "You two can go back if you want to, but I'm going on. Imagine her all alone in the dark and the storm!"

"I have no thought of turning back," Cousin William assured him. "If it gets so we can't find our way at all, we may have to stop until it blows over, but certainly we won't go back to Uphill Farm. Actually, we've reached the point of no return."

Willie shuddered and moaned softly, but they moved steadily on down the sodden trail. Another brilliant flash of lightning lit the forest some minutes later, and the Quaker uttered a delighted cry. In the brief instant of light, he had spotted a cabin just ahead of them.

"Friend John Minton's place!" he exclaimed. "And he's at home. There's light inside. We're much further along than I thought we were. We'll stop here and find out what he knows about Jo. She may even have taken shelter with him."

They drew their horses off the trail, and Cousin William went to the door. Friend Minton opened it immediately, and the warmth of candlelight and firelight streamed out into the night.

"Come in, come in, Friend William," he cried in amazement. "What brings thee into the forest on such a night?"

Cousin William beckoned the others to follow him, and they all tramped into the bright cabin. Mistress Minton, cheerful and pretty in her soft gray dress and white Quaker cap, surveyed them, dripping on her clean rag rugs, and threw up her hands in dismay.

"Thee is sopping wet!" she exclaimed. "Come to the fire and dry off, and I will give thee tea to warm thee."

George's intent eyes were darting into every corner of the tidy room.

"She isn't here," he mourned, half to himself.

Mistress Minton's quick ears caught the words.

"Who isn't here?" she asked, bustling about her tea-making.

George looked to Cousin William for help and the Quaker began the story, which he made as brief as possible.

"And so, you see," he concluded, "we're on our way

112

to Richard Harris' place to see if Josephine Charlotte is there. But with this dreadful storm, we doubt that she could have reached him yet, so we were very hopeful that she might have taken refuge with thee."

"She's not here, and we haven't seen anything of her," replied Friend John Minton. "We have been at home all day, and outside most of the time, so no one could have passed this way on the trail without our knowing it."

A troubled look came into his dark eyes.

"I think thee will be wasting thy time to go farther this way," he said slowly. "I am afraid thy young friend never arrived in this vicinity. Thee is aware, Friend William, of the men at work in the woods this summer?"

"Well aware," Cousin William nodded.

"Not more than a week ago," John Minton resumed, "a Negro man, about George's age, I would suppose, was on his way to the Susquehanna. All of the Quakers hereabouts were alerted and our servants were told to 'kill a sheep,' but he never appeared. We fear he has been kidnapped."

"What does it mean to 'kill a sheep?'" George asked.

Friend Minton smiled in spite of his concern.

"That simply means there is an escaped slave in the neighborhood, who is in need of food and shelter and will soon be crossing the river on Richard Harris' ferry," he explained. "When we tell them that, our people all keep their eyes open for him and offer help. This time we are afraid someone else got to him first."

Mistress Minton handed around steaming cups of tea and small sweet cakes. They all sipped in silence, and Cousin William finally voiced the fear in their minds.

"Does thee think we had best turn south now? Does thee know where their headquarters are? I have never known, for sure."

"We don't know for sure, either, Friend William," John Minton answered. "They keep on the move, thee knows. From some rumors we've heard lately we suspect they're over near Bush River now. It would be a logical place, for they have to find a mooring spot for their schooner, and that would be ideal. But mind, I'm not meaning I feel sure Josephine Charlotte has fallen into their hands; she may be lost, because thee says she was alone and unfamiliar with the woods, but I just think we should be prepared for the worst. More tea, please, Mistress."

Fresh tea was poured into their cups and they drank it, the wet travelers huddling close to the fire to dry their clammy clothes. Friend Minton brought out a pen-and-ink map of the forest, which they studied in the firelight.

"Thee was going north and somewhat east when thee came here," he said, pointing with a slender forefinger. "Now I think we had better retrace thy steps and turn south where the trail branches. Thee would not have seen the spot in the storm and darkness."

"Thee is not thinking of going with us!" Cousin William exclaimed. "This is not the night to be abroad unless thee has to; and besides, I think the fewer of us, the better, although I do thank thee."

"Of course I'm going," Friend Minton insisted. "If worse comes to worse and we should find the girl in their possession, two white men to engage the attention of the others while George and Willie go in to rescue her might be absolutely necessary."

"Me go in that place? *Me?*" demanded Willie, cowering back against the warm chimney. "Lordy no, I ain't going in no such place!"

Even George had to smile faintly.

Mistress Minton tried to persuade them to spend the rest of the night at the cabin and start out at daybreak, but only Willie was in favor of that, so still in their wet clothes they prepared to take their leave. Friend Minton put on a jacket and his broad-brimmed Quaker hat and went out to saddle a horse.

He lead them back along the wet trail, single file, with George bringing up the rear. The thunderstorm had rolled on, and the rain stopped. The clouds were breaking now, and an occasional star shone between them.

Their horses were moving along at a brisk walk and George felt better, in spite of Friend Minton's frank appraisal of Josephine Charlotte's situation. At least they were *doing* something, *getting* somewhere, not just creeping along the trail in the storm, not even knowing where they were going.

"Here's the fork," announced Friend Minton, suddenly. "We'll turn south here."

The rain had stopped entirely now, and moonlight and starlight began to filter down through the trees.

It was easier to see the trail, so they moved a little faster and came at last into a tiny clearing, bright with moonlight. It seemed a good place to rest for a few minutes, so they dismounted and let the horses graze on the wet grass. George walked about the little hollow to stretch his legs, wondering at the disheveled look of the small bramble bushes, and the torn turf.

"It looks trampled, Mr. William," he said, "as though animals had been fighting in here—a couple of bucks, maybe."

"I wouldn't be surprised, George," Cousin William agreed, absently. "Plenty of deer in these woods."

George was bending over one of the broken bramble bushes at the edge of the clearing and didn't answer; then he straightened up with something in his hand.

"This was caught on the bush," he said, trying to suppress his excitement.

Cousin William took a torn piece of cloth from George and examined it carefully.

"It certainly looks like cloth from a woman's dress!" he exclaimed.

Willie looked at it and let out a shout. "That's part of Josie's dress; I know it is. I seen her wear that brown calico time and agin. Josie's been here!"

"Hush! Keep the noise down," warned Friend Minton, coming over to look. "Thee can't be sure it's cloth from Josephine's dress. Thee can't see well enough in the moonlight. Not one chance in a thousand we'd come upon her trail so easily. This forest is so dense I've spent days searching for my cattle, even. Don't get thy hopes up."

116

George was down on his knees in the wet grass now, scrutinizing every inch of the torn turf.

"Look!" he cried. "No animal tore up that grass, Mr. William. It was dug up by feet, human feet. Can't you see those footprints where it's bare?"

Cousin William got down beside him and traced the marks in the wet earth carefully with his fingers. There were the prints of a woman's shoes and the bruising, heavy ones made by a man's big boots. Friend Minton looked at them closely, too. Then all three of them stood up and stared at each other.

"I apologize," said Friend Minton. "She could well have been here."

"I wish we had a hound dog for tracking," George said. "From the looks of things, she put up an awful fight, Mr. William. The marks are so deep even the rain didn't wash 'em out."

Willie was standing by. "If'n those kidnappers got Josie, how we gonna find them?" he wanted to know.

"We'll just push on the way we're going, down toward the Bush River," Friend Minton replied. "Evidently we're on the right track. It'll be too dark in the woods to see footprints, but we'll keep our eyes open, anyhow, and maybe there will be other signs. He may have taken her off into the woods farther, but he was surely going in the same direction as the trail. I feel sure the ship's anchored in the river not too far away, and wherever they keep the slaves must be a reasonable distance from it."

They were all back on their horses now, speaking in low voices, almost whispers, as though they expected the men to be within earshot. George was shaking inside with fury and apprehension. If they had hurt her! If they had already taken her aboard ship and away! They pressed on through the undergrowth, alert for the smallest sign that anyone had lately passed that way. Now and then they stopped their horses and listened, but all they could hear was the gentle soughing of the wind through the trees.

It seemed forever that they walked their horses through the forest, and George imagined the darkness was lifting and dawn was near. His fears were increased by the thought. If the boat were anchored in the river and the kidnappers planned to sail that night, they would have to get well out into the bay before daylight. He was frantic, thinking Josephine Charlotte might even at that moment be aboard the pirate ship.

"Let's hurry! Let's hurry!" he called to the Quakers.

"Thee must be patient," answered Friend Minton, calmly, reining his horse around a fallen branch. "Undue haste now could ruin our chances. I believe we are nearing the place where we may find them."

"I believe I hear a stream," Cousin William announced a few minutes later. "Stop and listen."

George heard it, too—the faint sound of water running near at hand.

"That should be James Run," said Friend Minton. "If so, I think we should leave the trail here and follow it, for it leads directly to the Bush River."

He turned his horse off into the deeper forest to the left of the trail, and the others followed, Willie protesting all the way. They rode slowly, straining their ears for the sound of running water, which grew clearer all the time.

"Here we are," called Friend Minton triumphantly.

There at their feet, flowing like black molten glass in the darkness, ran the little stream, pinpointed with flecks of starlight.

"There'll be no trouble finding the river now," Friend Minton declared with satisfaction. "We'll go along with our horses as far as Harford Furnace, and then we'll leave them in Willie's care and proceed on foot, the three of us. We will be much less apt to be apprehended."

"Oh no!" Willie objected. "I not a gonna stay with the horses."

"I thought thee didn't want to go with George to find Jo," said Cousin William.

"I don't," agreed Willie. "I ain't a gonna do neither one. I gonna stay with you."

"All right, we'll tie the horses," returned Cousin William. "We'll probably need all the men we have, anyhow."

Willie mumbled something unintelligible, and they pressed on. It wasn't long before Friend Minton called a halt, and they dismounted and tied the horses out of sight. Then they set out again, this time on foot, crawling through the undergrowth that edged the creek, moving as stealthily as Indians, not a word spoken. Finally Friend Minton put up his hand to beckon them all together.

"We're nearly there," he whispered. "Just a bit farther on we come to the place where James Run flows

119

into Bush River in a little cove. It's very secluded, and we Quakers have surmised that this is the place where they hide the schooner when they bring her up-river from the Chesapeake. There must be a cabin or shack of some kind close at hand where they keep their slaves until they're ready to ship them out."

The little run widened out as they crept along its banks, and suddenly they stopped as one man, for each had seen a small building against the darkness of the forest, ahead and to their left. They huddled together, not daring to make a move.

"No sign of life," whispered Cousin William. "Not even a guard."

"Isn't necessarily the place," Friend Minton whispered back. "Let's watch a while."

They squatted in the underbrush, scarcely breathing, for what seemed an eternity. Finally the unmistakable smell of tobacco floated to them on the damp air, and then a man coughed.

"The guard!" George whispered. "Let's attack now, before he knows anyone's around. Four against one."

"May be more than one," cautioned Friend Minton. "Better skirt the cabin and see what's below on the river. Must be more men somewhere, if this is the place."

At that moment they heard the faint scrape of a foot on a threshold and the sound of a door opening and closing. They crawled on their stomachs past the shanty as quickly as possible, although they were quite sure the guard had gone inside. When they were safely beyond it, they got to their feet and resumed their stealthy passage through the forest. The trees began to thin out, and they had to be even more cautious, darting from trunk to trunk and stopping close to each one for a moment.

Friend Minton mouthed a soundless warning, holding up his hand. Just ahead of them lay a clearing, and at its edge, glimmering in the waning moonlight, the Bush River lapped gently at the shore. Pacing back and forth in the pale light was another guard, rifle on his shoulder.

"D'you think there're just the two of them?" George asked.

"Very unlikely," returned Cousin William in an almost inaudible whisper.

They squatted in some thick bushes and tried to plan what to do. If there were only two men, it would be quite easy to overpower them, even though they were armed and the Quakers were not, but if more men were on the ship, which they assumed to be hidden in the cove, it would be a different matter. Finally the design began to take shape. The two Quakers would approach the clearing alone, feigning confusion during the storm, and asking the way to Abingdon. Meanwhile, the Negroes would reconnoiter at the shanty to see if there were a possible way in at the back where the guard wouldn't detect them.

"Now George," whispered Cousin William, turning toward him in the dim light, "you and Willie must be——"

His whisper trailed off in consternation. Willie wasn't there. He had been kneeling just in back of

George when they had huddled to confer. Now he was gone, and no one had heard or seen him go. He had simply vanished behind the screen of the forest.

"No more than I expected." George tried to express his great disgust in a whisper. "I'll manage without him, Mr. William."

He waited, ready to move as soon as the guard's attention was distracted. Cousin William and Friend Minton stood up and moved boldly out into the clearing. George saw the man whirl and level his rifle at them in a single fluid move. Each Quaker raised a hand in protest and advanced calmly toward him.

"Peace, friend," Cousin William intoned in his most tranquil Quaker inflections. "We come unarmed; thee has nought to fear from us. We merely seek directions to Abingdon and a chance to rest here in the clearing for a little time. We lost our way in the forest during the storm, and coming from over Fallston way we have little knowledge of the trails in these parts."

The guard lowered his rifle, and George didn't wait to hear any more. He was off, crawling on all fours through the thick underbrush toward the shanty. He was so afraid of making a betraying sound that he scarcely breathed on his perilous way past the front of the rickety building. Once near the back he relaxed a little and moved faster. The big question in his mind was whether or not the guard at the shanty was armed. If not, he stood a good chance of overpowering him. The man was outside again, sitting on the step smoking his pipe; George had seen his silhouette as he crept by, but he still couldn't be sure if a rifle lay beside him, or a pistol hung from his belt.

At the back of the cabin George stood up cautiously, surveying the wall in front of him. Surely there must be some opening other than the door to let in light and air. There it was, a small window barred with a grillwork made of wooden slats. What luck! He felt carefully, but found no glass under his fingers. He pulled tentatively, and the wood gave just enough to make his pulse jump; if it were old enough and rotten enough, he could tear it away with his fingers. Instantly he heard a sound from inside the shanty—a faint clanking of a chain and a mutter. People were in there. George on an impulse put his mouth close to the bars and whispered,

"Jo, are you there?"

He knew he had taken a tremendous risk—one loud exclamation from a prisoner and all would be lost— but his question was greeted only by silence. Then came the answer he awaited so tensely.

"George? Oh, George!"

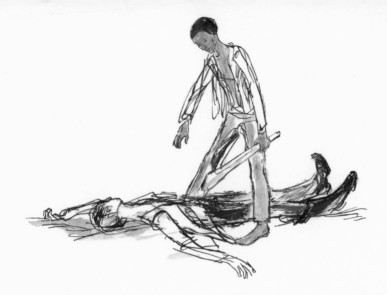

chapter 13

THE QUIET OF the night was suddenly torn by
sounds of shouting and violence. George dropped
to the ground as though he had been shot and lay
there panting until he heard the thud of running feet
down the path to the clearing and guessed that the
shanty guard had gone to investigate. Then he leaped
to his feet and tore the bars from the window. He
pulled himself up to the sill and dived head first into
the room below, landing spread eagle across the laps of
three Negroes who sat on the floor with their fettered
legs out in front of them. As he picked himself up, the
shanty seemed pitch dark; but after a moment or two

of fumbling about, his eyes adjusted and he could make out Josephine Charlotte in the gloom. She made a pitiful gesture toward him with her bound hands. He crawled to her and gathered her into his arms, feeling how she flinched when he touched her back.

"You're hurt!" he whispered fiercely.

"He whipped me when I tried to run," she explained. "But don't bother now. Take me away!"

George already had his sharp jackknife out and was cutting the ropes that bound her hands and feet.

"Thank God they're ropes!" he breathed. "Got to get you out of here before the guard gets back!"

The last one was cut and he was lifting her up when they heard the running feet of the guard rushing back to the shanty. George dragged her across the bodies of the fettered Negroes to the window and without a word heaved her up and head first over the sill, letting her fall onto the wet ground below. He crawled back to the empty place where she had been sitting and barely had time to settle into it when the door was flung open and the white man leaped into the room.

"Armed?" George hissed into the ear of the prisoner next to him.

"Pistol," he whispered back.

George stiffened against the wall. He was counting on a few seconds of grace while the guard's eyes adjusted to the gloom. The man stood in the middle of the tiny room, struggling to see in the faint light. He swung around to the wall where George was sitting in the place once occupied by Josephine Charlotte. George prayed that he wouldn't detect the difference in the black face, but he did.

"Where's the woman?" he screamed, bounding into the air and grabbing the pistol from his belt. In the split second before he had a chance to level it, George catapulted himself at the huge man, striking the pistol from his hand and propelling him toward the door. He had to get out of the cramped space, filled with helpless men in chains. The man was beginning to recover from the shock of George's attack. He was tall and massive, more than a match for George in every way. Soon they were out in front of the cabin, fighting silently. George's right eye was soon closed and the left nearly blinded with the blood that ran into it from a cut on his forehead.

He wondered, as they plunged and reeled, how long he could keep it up and what had become of the Quakers and Willie. A bitter resentment welled up inside of him when he thought of Willie, hiding somewhere in the forest. And where had Jo gone after he'd flung her out of the window? Had she hidden herself far enough away so the guard couldn't find her if he won the fight? Had she been hurt by the fall?

He was moving slowly now, his blows weakening, staggering in his fatigue; his head felt like a ball of cotton; he couldn't think much longer. He went down under a crushing assault from the bull of a man, and lay there, too exhausted to struggle to his feet any more, awaiting the final blow, his eyes shut.

Suddenly something came crashing through the bushes in front of the shanty; he heard a series of thwacking sounds, and then a mighty, crunching noise and a grunt. There was silence, and George cautiously opened his one good eye and peered up at Willie standing over him, waving a stout club and grinning. One foot was firmly planted on the immense chest of the fallen giant.

"Git up, George," Willie ordered, "an' git somepin' to tie this white man up with. I don' wanna stan' here forever."

"What happened," George demanded, staggering dizzily to his feet and moving his arms and legs experimentally. "And where have you been?"

"Git this fella tied up," Willie repeated. "I tell you all about it after a while."

George went into the shanty and brought out the ropes that had bound Josephine Charlotte; he tied the guard securely, and Willie hauled him over and propped him up against the doorstep. The man was coming to now, shouting oaths at both of them. They turned their backs on him and left him. The fog was beginning to clear from George's brain.

"First of all we have to find Jo," he remembered, starting off around the corner of the shack.

"Find Jo?" cried Willie. "You mean she ain' in there, after all this? You mean I did all this for nothin'?"

"I pushed her out of the window just before that monster came in," George explained. "I hope she didn't break something when she fell, but I had to get her out of there."

He stood at the back of the cabin, peering into the forest. Behind him he could hear talk from the shackled Negroes and calls for help, but first he had to find Jo.

"Jo," he called, "Josephine Charlotte, where are you?"

Willie stood beside him, and they waited for some sign of her presence. George began to think of the other guard and the probability of more men in the gang.

"Maybe she'd better stay in the woods," he said. "I forgot about the others. We'll have to go and help Mr. William and Friend Minton."

Willie was grinning again, a wide, happy grin.

"Don' you pay no attention to them Quaker gen' men," he said. "They all right. You go git Josie an' we find them an' you hears all about it."

There was a sound in the bushes just beyond the cabin, they parted and Josephine Charlotte stuck her head out. Her face was stained with tears and scratched by brambles; her beautiful black hair was tousled, and her eyes were frantic with fear. When she saw Willie, she turned to run back into the woods again, but George reached her in one stride and took her hand gently.

"Don't be afraid," he murmured, stroking her hair. "It's all over, and you're safe with us. Willie told us all about it, and he came with us to find you. You don't need to be afraid of him any more. Cousin William came with us, and a friend of his, a Quaker named John Minton."

Josephine Charlotte was looking in bewilderment from George to Willie and back to George again.

"Are you trying to tell me that Master Robert didn't ever plan to sell me and that I didn't have to marry Willie?" she demanded.

"No, you didn't have to, and you aren't going to," George assured her.

Josephine Charlotte turned suddenly and furiously on Willie.

"I loathe you, Willie," she cried. "I loathe you with all the strength I have, and I shall loathe you as long as I live!"

Willie stood looking at her with his great hands limp at his sides. George thought he was going to cry.

"I didn' mean to make trouble like this, Josie," he said in a half whimper. "Hones' I never meant to do it. I jes' wanted you to marry with me; an' after George came I could see you was fallin' in love with him, an' I had to do somepin' quick. It didn' work the way I planned. You run off, an' then I knowed I was wrong. I been so scared, Josie. D'you think you can forgive me sometime?"

Josephine Charlotte had been listening to him, but there was contempt still smoldering in her dark eyes.

"I don't know whether I can forgive you, ever," she declared. "Do you realize I was going to be shipped down the coast to Georgia this very night if Cousin William and George hadn't come? Do you know that my back is covered with slashes from that horrible man's whip? Look, my dress is sticking to it."

She turned so that they could see the blood turned black that had oozed onto her old calico dress.

"How can you ask me to forgive you, Willie?" she

wailed, and burst into tears in George's arms.

George noted the stricken look on Willie's face and kissed the tears away from Josephine Charlotte's eyes.

"Now, now!" he soothed her. "I didn't think I could forgive him either, Jo, but not more than ten minutes ago he saved my life, so I guess I can forgive him after all."

"Oh," said Josephine Charlotte.

She looked intently at Willie's melancholy face and the angry lines smoothed out of her own.

"Ask me again tomorrow, Willie," she suggested. "It's all too fresh right now."

She was limping a little and hung onto George's arm as they walked around the cabin.

"Maybe I'll have to think about forgiving you, too, George," she said, smiling a little. "I twisted my ankle when you tossed me out of the window."

They passed the bound guard, still hurling oaths into the dawn, and went on down to the clearing to find Cousin William and Friend Minton.

"I leave 'em there," explained Willie, "an' come a-runnin' when I hear you in trouble, George."

They were there, each gentleman standing straight and stern in his gray clothes and his broad-brimmed Quaker hat, each one holding a long rifle in his hand, pointed straight at two white men sitting on the ground, hands held high above their heads. As the three approached, Cousin William was saying politely to the ringleader of the gang, the very man who had attempted to abduct Jo in Baltimore,

"I regret to tell thee that if thee moves so much as

one inch, I shall not hesitate to shoot thee with thy own gun."

The rifle shook in Friend Minton's hand, but he dared not turn his shocked look upon Cousin William, so he stared fixedly at the kidnapper he guarded as he rebuked his friend,

"Friend William, thee knows what the Scripture says: 'Thou shalt not kill,' and also 'He that liveth by the sword shall perish by the sword.' How can thee in cold blood say to this poor man, '. . . I shall not hesitate to shoot thee?' "

"Poor man, indeed!" snorted Cousin William. "Thee did not see him attempting to abduct Josephine Charlotte in Baltimore not a week ago. I did not mean that I would shoot to kill him, but I would shoot to injure him, and I have no doubt that would be very painful indeed."

The leader of the gang rolled his eyes apprehensively toward the muzzle of the rifle, keeping his hands high.

"Don't shoot," he implored. "If you ever pull that trigger, the way you handle that rifle, I'm a goner."

George bit his lip to restrain a grin and moved toward the Quakers.

"Let me hold the gun, Mr. William," he suggested, "and you search your man for keys to the handcuffs and fetters on the men in the shack. We'll get them off right away."

A few minutes later, keys in hand, he and Willie left to release the prisoners; and Josephine Charlotte sat down on the grass close to Cousin William, who had resumed his guard duties. The sun was rising now, turning Bush River a pale, shimmering blue, and she wondered what had become of the pirate ship she knew had been hidden in the cove. She still trembled at the nearness of the kidnappers and shuddered to think of her fate if help had not come.

Cousin William sensed her agitation and spoke to her softly,

"Jo, thee has had a bad, bad time of it. I can see blood stains on thy dress and scratches on thy face, but they will heal. Thee must calm thyself now and realize that because of thee all of these men will be released and able to go free again."

"I suppose so," she nodded. "All of them but one are free Negroes, and it was horrible for them to think of being sold again into slavery. But one was an escaped slave. What will happen to him?"

"Just as we thought!" exclaimed Friend Minton. "That's the one I was telling thee about, Friend William."

"He will have his chance," Cousin William assured Josephine. "That's only fair, doesn't thee think?"

"I do think," she agreed.

"When George and Willie return with the others, we will use some of their shackles to restrain these amiable fellows, and then we will hear everybody's story as we journey back to Uphill Farm. The sooner we get thee back there the better. Miss Sarah and Mistress Elizabeth are terribly upset. It has been bad for the mistress at this time," the Quaker said.

"I know," Jo agreed. "I worried about Mistress

Elizabeth when I was in the woods."

She sighed and looked uneasily over her shoulder at the river.

"What has become of the schooner?" she asked. "Are you *sure* the crew won't come here to get me now?"

Cousin William smiled. "Don't worry," he said. "The crisis is over. Before dawn the schooner weighed anchor and set sail; we saw it move out of its hiding place in the cove and head south. Obviously the sailors, brave fellows, heard the sounds of struggle and departed. As soon as these men, who were the leaders of the gang, are safely bound, Friend Minton will ride down the coast and notify the authorities. We hope they can be headed off and captured, too."

Josephine Charlotte nodded with relief, and just at that moment George and Willie appeared from the woods with the Negro men at their heels, limping and walking stiffly because they had been bound for several days. But everyone was beaming with happiness.

"Now let's go home!" cried Josephine Charlotte.

"Not so fast," said George, handcuffing the prisoners. "While I get these men anchored here tell me, where did Willie come from? I thought he ran away. And how did you gentlemen overpower the kidnappers, they being armed, and all?"

"Well," answered Cousin William, "I really should let Willie tell you because it's his story, but I want to tell you myself. I'm afraid he might be too modest. This is what happened: Willie did run off, as you know, because he was really frightened, but he didn't go far. He was hiding in the woods when he heard the commotion down here. The leader of the gang was returning from the ship and heard us, er, hoodwinking the guard. He immediately recognized me as the one who had deprived him of Jo at the slave market in Baltimore and began shouting that we weren't seeking directions but had come after her again. You must have heard the noise."

"Yes, I did," said George. "I was just about to climb in the cabin window when it happened."

"Then Willie came slinking out of the woods with a huge cudgel in his hand," Cousin William resumed. "The men had their backs to him and were all ready to shoot us, I fear, when he leaped upon them with his club and knocked them unconscious. That's all there was to it, but I never expect to see any man do a braver thing—two armed professional criminals, and one man with only a club!"

Willie hung his head. "Twasn't really nothin'," he muttered. "I jes' wanted to git Josie out a there."

"That isn't all," added George. "With that same club he saved my life, too. I guess all of us would have been dead, and Jo on her way to Georgia by now, if it hadn't been for Willie."

Willie raised his head and looked straight into Josephine Charlotte's eyes.

"I guess it was me made all the trouble in the first place," he said. "So 'twas only fitten for me to do somepin'."

chapter 14

IT WAS NOON when George rode out of the shadows of the forest trail, holding Josephine Charlotte in front of him on the horse. Exhaustion from her long ordeal had set in, and she drooped against him, scarcely aware they were riding up the drive to the big house. They were alone now; the free Negroes, one after the other, had dropped out of the procession to go to their little farms in the clearings; and the escaped slave had faded into the depths of the forest while the rest of the party discreetly looked the other way. Cousin William and Willie had gone to Bel Air to turn their prisoners over to the sheriff. It all seemed an incredible dream to her, now, and the scene that greeted them as they rounded the last curve was part of the unreality.

Master Robert was cantering up to the house on his favorite dapple-gray, with a band of mounted men following him. Mr. Harry on his big bay, was there, too. Benjy, Jim, and Corbin were dancing around excitedly. The doctor's gig was standing in the drive, and Josephine Charlotte gave a little gasp of alarm when she saw it. At that moment Sarah came running out of the house, not seing them at first.

"It's a girl, Papa! It's a girl!" she screamed.

Master Robert leaped from his horse and rushed into the house, and then everyone seemed to notice the new arrivals at the same time. George slid from the saddle and lifted Josephine to the ground. Sarah rushed to her, crying out her joy,

"Jo, Jo! I've been so terribly worried. Thank heaven!"

"The baby came!" Josephine Charlotte cried, brushing aside Sarah's excitement over her, "How's the mistress?"

"Fine," Sarah assured her. "But *you*? Oh, Jo!"

She held her off to look at her, and then she caught a glimpse of the dried blood stains on the back of the bedraggled brown calico dress.

"That's blood on your dress!" she cried in horror. "How did it *get* there?"

She touched the stains timidly with her fingers and burst into tears. Tears began to gather in Josephine's eyes, too, so George walked toward them to inter-

136

vene.

"Jo is too tired to tell about it now, Miss Sarah," he said "I'll tell you what happened after she's taken care of, and then you can talk about it together later. She needs to get that dress off, and her cuts washed, and to have a good rest. She hasn't slept for two nights, or had a meal."

"Of course," cried Sarah. "I just didn't think. Come on upstairs and let me fix your back."

She urged her gently up the steps, but Jo protested. "After I get washed up and my dress changed and something to eat, I'll be fine. No time to sleep now with a new baby in the house!"

She attempted a bright smile and a gay manner, but Sarah saw through her.

"Don't worry about the baby," she said. "She has more people wanting to take care of her than one baby can use. Mary Ann and Ellen are up there fussing over her now, and Aunt Mattie and the doctor are with Mama. You're going straight to bed after you've had some tea."

They met Master Robert coming downstairs, beaming over his new daughter. He was amazed to see Josephine Charlotte and wanted to talk to her at once, but Sarah persuaded him to let George tell about it, so the girls proceeded up the stairs. Mary Ann and Ellen met them at the top, full of excited questions, but Sarah brushed them off.

"Later," she said briefly, leading Jo down the hall to their room. "Go and get some hot tea and something for her to eat if you want to help."

"Can't I see Mistress and the baby for a minute?" Josephine begged as they passed the closed door to her room.

"Later," Sarah said firmly. "The doctor's still here, anyhow." She pushed her through the door to their room and shut it after them.

Then for the first time in their lives, the roles of mistress and maid were reversed, and it was Sarah who gently helped Jo out of her dress and bathed the torn back, shuddering. Sarah put a clean nightdress on Jo and turned down not the trundle bed with the hard straw tick, but the four-poster with the feather bed. She insisted that Jo climb in, and she propped her up with pillows so that she could eat the fresh bread and jelly and drink the good hot tea that Sarah's sisters brought. The three girls stood and watched her eating hungrily, refraining from asking the dozens of questions that rose to their lips. But Josephine Charlotte had one of her own, before she gingerly wriggled down in the soft bed.

"Where was the master going with all those men?" she asked.

Mary Ann told her. "Papa waited as long as he could stand it; and when Cousin William didn't bring you back this morning, he sent Mr. Harry for all the neighbors to form a posse and go out to help look for you. Papa wasn't sheriff all that time for nothing."

Josephine Charlotte smiled a pleased little smile and closed her eyes. Before the girls had tiptoed out of the room she was asleep. It was early evening when she awoke. She could tell by the shadows that filled the room and the clatter of dishes being washed in the kitchen. The high-pitched cry of the newborn child came to her. She crawled stiffly down from the high bed, feeling infinitely better, and went to wash her face and get dressed.

In a few minutes she stood peeking in the door of the mistress' room. Mistress Elizabeth was awake and delighted to see her.

"Come in and see our new baby, and tell me what happened to you," she urged.

Josephine Charlotte took the baby from her mother's arms and cooed over her.

"She's beautiful!" she exclaimed. "Look at all that hair! What's her name?"

"Ann. I've always wanted to name a baby Ann," said the mistress. "And I suspect this may be our last, so Ann is going to be her name. But now, Jo, you sit down and hold her and tell me everything that happened in the woods. I've just heard little bits and pieces; I guess they were afraid of upsetting me. I know how George rescued you, and what a hero Willie was, but nobody told me how you were kidnapped in the first place. You tell me. I want to hear it from you, if you can bear to talk about it."

Josephine Charlotte sat down on the foot of the bed, the tiny, soft bundle cradled in her arms, and began. She told about her first terrifying night in the woods, her fear lest she not find the right trail, and her alarm over the animals prowling through the night, which really made her lose her way.

"Why?" asked the mistress, hanging on every word.

"Well, toward the end of the night," Josephine Charlotte continued, "I was very tired of walking and so frightened, and all of a sudden I thought some kind of animal was stalking me. When I looked around, I could see its eyes glowing in the dark, and I began to run and scream. I must have scared it away. But about that time I came to a fork in the trail, and I guess I turned the wrong way—anyhow I was in such a panic that I ran and ran as long as I could. Then the sun started to come up, and I found out I had gone in the wrong direction. By that time I was about dead, and afraid I'd be seen, so when I found this tiny clearing, I curled up and went to sleep behind some bushes."

"Was that the place George found the piece of your dress?" the mistress asked.

Josephine nodded. "That was the place. A noise woke me up, and there was that horrible man standing over me—the one I saw in Baltimore. He took hold of me and started dragging me out of the clearing. I began to struggle and fight and tore my dress on the brambles, and he got awfully mad and whipped me with a branch he pulled off a bush."

She began to tremble as she told the story, and the mistress shuddered. Jo noticed her agitation and said quickly,

"I must go now. You're getting too tired."

"No, no!" protested Mistress Elizabeth. "I want to hear it all, and then we'll all try to forget it and just be thankful you're safe."

So Josephine Charlotte hurried on, leaving out parts she thought might be too harrowing. Sarah came in softly and sat on the other side of the bed. Josephine told how she was finally dragged to the dreadful, putrid little shack, bound with ropes, hand and foot, and propped against the wall with the other Negroes who had been stolen.

All the long, hot day they sat there, unable to move, suffering terribly because they were given no water, not to mention food, and not allowed to talk. Whenever anyone made a sound the guard came in and threatened them all with his gun. She told about the dreadful night, with the great storm, and about hearing the leader tell the guard the ship was dropping anchor in the cove.

It wasn't necessary for her to describe the blackness of her despair.

"Didn't you know George would try to find you?" demanded Miss Sarah.

"Well, I thought he might try," Josephine admitted, smiling a little. "But I didn't think he could do it. And besides, he might actually have thought it was best for me to get away. I had no idea Willie would tell why I left."

"Thanks to Cousin William and Friend Minton, and George's own persistence he did find you," sighed Miss Sarah happily, "and we have you home again, safe and sound, and Mama knows the rest of the story."

Jo nodded, and then she added, hesitantly, "It's so strange, but Willie helped an awful lot, too."

chapter 15

JOSEPHINE CHARLOTTE had expected life to settle down into its old grooves within a few days. A sound night's sleep did restore her body to its usual vigor, but the buoyant spirit that usually went with it was much slower in coming back. In fact, she began to wonder if it ever would. As she sat, day after day, sewing on Sarah's blue velvet pelisse, she pondered the feeling of melancholy that had enveloped her while she was a prisoner in the shack and still lingered, now that she was safe at home. At first she supposed it would go away after the raw vividness of the time faded.

"My thoughts will heal with my back," she said to herself, setting the perfect stitches in the soft velvet.

The ugly cuts healed with the passing days, though they left scars that would last as long as she lived, but the mood of depression clung around her like an invisible cloud. She decided that it must be invisible to the people in the household, for even Sarah, always so alert to her feelings, seemed not to notice. Josephine Charlotte was glad, because Sarah had at last abandoned herself to the joy of her coming marriage. Jo was sure she had never been so pretty. She flitted about the house, radiantly happy, trying on the magnificent satin wedding gown at Miss Minnie's call, or stopping to love the baby and chat with her mother, or sitting beside Jo as she made the cherished velvet pelisse.

"I'm always going to keep it, Jo," she said earnestly one day as Josephine was turning up the hem. She turned carefully on command as Jo put in the pins, smoothing the luscious length of the skirt with her hands. "No matter what happens in life to either one of us, I'll have this to remember you by."

Josephine Charlotte recoiled inwardly, as though she had been pushed close to the edge of an abyss and were teetering there. Miss Sarah's remark was casual, but it released all the pent-up fears in Jo's mind. No longer did she have to worry about marrying Willie, but the question that had sprung into her mind weeks ago and had faded into the background emerged as the true focal point of her unrest: "Josephine Charlotte— what of Josephine Charlotte?"

Her future loomed ahead of her, bleak and uncertain; her worry about it could no longer be suppressed. Too many awful things could happen.

That night as she sat with George on the grass in the back of the kitchen quarters, she tried to analyze her feelings.

"Of course, I'm not stupid enough to believe that all this happened in those two days," she mused. "At first I thought I could trace this change in my feelings back to the slave market in Baltimore. Everything I saw there affected me so much—I didn't know things like that existed: the young slave being sold, and the mother crying for her baby."

She shuddered and moved closer to him. He put his arm around her, and she continued.

"But I'm sure now that wasn't the beginning. Something Miss Sarah said to me today brought it all back to me like a flash. The night Mr. Harry proposed to her, I overheard Master Robert saying how poor the tobacco was and that he guessed he'd have to sell some Negroes before winter. That was it—I realized right then that no matter how kind your master was, or how happy you thought you were, if you were a slave to some other human, you could be *sold*. From that minute on I don't suppose I've had any time when I really felt safe."

"But you didn't think then that he meant to sell *you*, did you, Jo?" George asked.

"Well, not exactly," she replied, "but you can't ever be *sure* again, once you get that thought in your head. It hides in there and pops out when you don't expect it. Oh, don't you see what I mean? You just can't ever be sure your happiness is going to last."

"Well," mused George, "I don't 'spose white folks can always be sure their happiness is going to last, either, as far as that goes. People get sick and die, or move away, or get mad and fight with each other. Lots of them have bad trouble."

"I know," Josephine Charlotte nodded, "but that's just being a human. Everybody has that kind. On top of it, we have all these other things. You know very well that we can never do what we please. We always have to do what somebody else pleases, and then there's always that awful feeling that you might be sold and your whole life would be just torn up by the roots. No, George, the more I think about it, the more I'm sure Mr. William was dead right when he said to me, 'No human being should *ever* be owned by another!'"

"That's a nice idea, all right," George agreed, "but when does he think that's going to happen?"

"He doesn't know for sure," Jo answered, "but he said to me, the way he talks, you know, 'It *will* come. It *must* come.' And the first time I heard him say it was when I was little and he was talking to my granny. He said, '. . . perhaps when thy little Jo, here, is grown up.'"

They sat in silence for a few minutes, breathing the sweetness that came from the garden on the gentle evening wind. Aunt Mattie walked by on her way to the slave quarters and cast a searching glance in their direction. They heard laughter from the veranda where

145

Mr. Harry and Miss Sarah sat, chaperoned by assorted sisters in the absence of Mistress Elizabeth.

"One good thing about being a slave," George said, laughing, "nobody bothers sitting with us when we're keeping company."

Josephine Charlotte laughed, too. "You saw the look Aunt Mattie gave us, didn't you? She considers that doing her duty as a chaperone."

She nestled in the curve of George's arm and laid her head on his shoulder.

"Oh dear," she murmured, "I wish I knew what to do!"

George turned his head to answer, softly, close to her ear,

"Josephine, my love, there is just one thing for you to do—stop your worrying. We're going to see that Miss Sarah and Mr. Harry get married proper, and then one day soon you and I are going to be married, too—just like the white folks, with a minister and all. You do love me, Jo, don't you? You do want to marry me? That's all I've been able to think about ever since I first saw you that day in the pretty green dress. I want you to wear that dress on our wedding day."

He held her away from him and sought for his answer in her beautiful face, warm and dark in the pink twilight. No answer came—just a look of anguish too deep to be borne—so he hid her face against him and smoothed her curls with his hand. Finally she looked up into those glowing dark eyes and tried to explain.

"Think of what I've just been saying to you,

George. Think! How can I marry you, knowing that some day, having borne your child, it might be snatched from me, or both the child and I might be sold away from you? I love you, I love you! But I——."

"*Don't!*" he commanded her, holding his hand tight against her mouth. "I will never let you say 'no' to me."

He took his hand away and pressed his mouth against hers. The kiss was long, and when it was done, it had said all that either needed to say to the other.

After that night Josephine Charlotte hid in her heart the bitter happiness she dared not acknowledge. The days before Sarah's wedding flew by, and the blue velvet pelisse was finished and hung away in all its smartness, to await the coming of the Maryland winter. Josephine Charlotte was promoted to the task of helping Miss Minnie with the finishing touches on the wedding gown.

"You make those tiny little tucks on the bodice, Jo," suggested Miss Minnie. "Your stitches are so perfect, and my old eyes can't see to do them so well anymore."

Josephine was delighted; it was sheer joy to handle the superb white satin and to set row after row of minute tucks below the filmy lace yoke. Miss Minnie had designed it beautifully, she thought, as she sat in the sewing room stitching away, listening to the voluble old seamstress' chatter.

"That velvet pelisse looks positively professional, Jo," she said admiringly. "I couldn't have done it better myself."

"I don't think I could have done it without you, Miss Minnie," Josephine Charlotte said modestly.

"Oh yes," Miss Minnie insisted. "I was so busy with this gown that I didn't do much for you with the pelisse—just gave you a few ideas; you did practically all the designing and all of the fitting yourself. Everybody in Harford County will wonder where little Mrs. Harry got her beautiful new outfit when she wears it next winter, and that little fur bonnet is adorable. You know, really, somebody should set you up in the dressmaking business. You've got natural talent, girl. You could make a fortune in the city."

She looked at Josephine Charlotte appraisingly; and then, as though she realized suddenly that she was talking to a slave, she stopped abruptly and actually sewed in silence for a few minutes. Josephine Charlotte nodded her thanks, as her own thoughts jumped from the pleasure of creating to the bitter futility of her position. Through the open window she heard the sound of an arrival at the veranda steps and hurried to look down. There was Uncle Corbin getting out of the carriage, embracing Sarah, instructing Jonas about his luggage, kissing the mistress as she sat holding the baby.

"How's the bride," he boomed in his great, hearty voice, "and the new little mother? Is this one number ten or eleven, Elizabeth? Boy or girl? Mighty pretty, no matter which. The stage was right on the dot in Bel Air, and there was Jonas waiting for me. Is that beautiful wedding gown done? Take me to see it, Sarah."

Almost before Josephine Charlotte was back at her stitching, Uncle Corbin was striding into the room with Sarah, greeting them and admiring the gown extravagantly.

"Beautiful, beautiful!" he exclaimed. "How smart you are to have such accomplished people doing your trousseau. Now let me see the blue velvet one. Did Josephine Charlotte get it done, what with her unfortunate mishap in the woods and all? Jonas told me about it on the way over."

Jo went to get it and held it up for his inspection.

"Magnificent!" he approved. "What good taste, Sarah, my dear. Lovely material and such a fine design. Half the ladies in Baltimore would envy you that."

"Really, Uncle Corbin," Sarah protested, her cheeks flaming with embarrassment, "I didn't have a thing to do with it. It was all Jo's doing."

"Well, I doubt that," said Uncle Corbin gallantly, "but even if it was, you were the smart one to pick such a gal, wasn't she, Jo?"

He pinched Sarah's cheek and marched her out of the room before anyone had a chance to reply. Josephine Charlotte went on placing the wee stitches in the satin, wondering if she would ever grow used to the hurts that came to her so often from insensitive people.

Only two days were left before the wedding. Uncle Corbin was already here, and Cousin William would ride over on his tall gray horse almost any time now. Josephine Charlotte found herself very eager to see him again. George was here almost every day, helping Willie groom the garden for the wedding. It was George who built a lovely little arch for the bridal couple, painted it white, and planned to twine it with sweet pea vines and crepe myrtle blossoms on the wedding day.

Aunt Mattie was commanding a busy staff in the kitchen, baking the wedding cake and cooking many special dishes for the wedding supper. Mouthwatering smells wafted into the house where the rest of the Negro house servants and the older girls in the family were cleaning and polishing and decorating. Mary Ann and Ellen had the task of arranging the flowers, so they were cutting armfuls of rosebuds and daisies and foxglove and other garden flowers and putting them in buckets of water in the spring house. The morning of the wedding, before the neighbors and relatives began to arrive, they would put them in vases and bowls and the big house would smell like a garden.

Miss Minnie and Josephine Charlotte were frantically putting the finishing touches on the wedding gown, calling Sarah every little while to try it on "just once more." She declared it was the most beautiful gown she had ever seen, and Jo assured her she would be the most beautiful bride anyone had ever seen. It would be a simple wedding, just Sarah and Mr. Harry walking together in the garden to stand in front of the preacher and say their vows.

The men were setting up tables on the lawn; and after the wedding, supper would be served in the warm twilight. Josephine Charlotte could picture it all now, the dancing and the singing and Sarah flitting among them in her lovely white gown. She would have white roses in her golden curls, and in her arms.

The wedding day dawned perfectly clear and hot. Carriages began to roll up the long, curving drive before noon, with ladies alighting at the horse block, lifting their long, full skirts daintily. The family came from miles around—even her grandmother and grandfather came from Fox Hill Farm for the day, and the neighbors arrived later, all of them bringing gifts for the young couple. Mistress Elizabeth sat in a chair on the veranda, presiding over the proceedings, and laughing and chatting. Jo decided it was a good thing, after all, that little Ann had arrived before she was expected.

Cousin William rode over from Fallston during the afternoon. Josephine Charlotte saw him come, but she was far too busy to seek him out for a talk, and besides, what did she have to say to him, and what could he say to her?

The sun was setting now, a vast red ball rolling away beyond the gentle Maryland hills. Josephine Charlotte fastened the last tiny satin button on Sarah's gown and handed her the sweet bouquet of white roses. She had fastened a cluster of them in the curls on top of Sarah's head, and now Sarah stood and looked at her for a moment, silently.

"Jo," she faltered, "I'm going to be married! I can't stop, now. I can't turn back, Jo."

Panic trembled in her voice, and Josephine Charlotte took command.

"Mr. Harry is waiting for you," she said gently, but with the fiber of firmness underneath. "You must go down now, and don't forget that you *love* him, Miss Sarah."

Sarah looked long and searchingly into the strong, dark face. Josephine Charlotte went to the door and opened it. Sarah straightened her shoulders and lifted her head; she went through it and down the winding stairs to the wide, dim hall where Mr. Harry waited for her. He took her hand, and they walked out into the softness of the evening. Josephine Charlotte followed and stood beside George on the lawn where the Negroes watched, at a distance from the white people. She glanced up to see Willie moving up to stand on her other side.

A deep quiet had settled over Uphill Farm, the chatter and the laughter had ceased. Mr. Harry and Miss Sarah walked slowly through the garden, her long satin gown trailing on the grassy path to the flower-decked arch where the preacher from the Old Brick Baptist Church waited for them. As they murmured their marriage vows, twilight covered them softly, as though it were a misty veil, tinted gold by the last pale shafts of sunlight. It rested on Miss Sarah's face as the preacher's deep voice proclaimed the solemn, ancient words: "I pronounce you man and wife."

Josephine Charlotte watched and breathed a soft sigh of relief. There was no panic in Miss Sarah's face now, only an indescribable happiness. A strange little sound came from her right, and she looked up at Willie. He was wiping his face with a clean handkerchief, and when he felt her glance on him he turned away; so Josephine Charlotte knew she could do nothing to help, and she found it possible to be sorry.

Miss Sarah and her husband, smiling after the preacher's blessing, turned to be kissed by her mother and father and the girls. Uncle Corbin boomed out his congratulations, kissing the bride and pounding the groom on the back. Cousin William came to take her gently into his arms and give his best wishes. Candles were lighted on the long tables and they burned steadily, for even the winds were still for Miss Sarah's wedding. Food was brought, and punch in great silver bowls. Mary Ann and Ellen ladled punch for everyone, and the glasses were raised in a toast to Sarah and Harry.

Sarah was too excited to eat, but she and Mr. Harry cut the beautiful wedding cake and then sat down to open presents. A great golden harvest moon sailed up over the trees to light the garden. Several Negro men began to strum on their banjos and draw the bow across their fiddles, so the dancing and the singing began. It was late in the night before it was done and people talked reluctantly of going home. Then Master Robert stood in an open place on the lawn and held up his hand for silence. The noise died away, and Josephine Charlotte drew close to George in the deep shadows where they had been watching.

"Before any of you go home," the master's big voice rumbled on the warm night air, "there is one more present to be given to my daughter, Sarah, on her wedding night. Her mama and I want her to have a gift that we believe she will cherish more than any other of the splendid gifts she has received. Because Sarah and her maid, Josephine Charlotte, have been together in a very special relationship ever since they were little tykes, we feel they should be together now that Sarah is about to leave our home for one of her own. So Josephine is our gift to you, my dear." He raised his voice, "Josie, where are you?"

Josephine Charlotte pressed close to George's side, trembling with an emotion she could not define. At last it had come this event for which in time gone by she had longed so passionately, and now she thought she could not make herself move out into the circle of brilliant moonlight where Master Robert awaited her with his arm around his daughter. Suddenly Cousin William was beside her, materializing from the shadows.

"Go on, dear child," he said softly but firmly. "This is expected of you. Go for Miss Sarah's sake."

She obeyed him at once, moving toward Miss Sarah as in a dream. Master Robert reached out and took her hand and held it out to Sarah.

"She's yours, daughter, from this day on. Later I shall see that you have the necessary papers," he said heartily.

Cheers and clapping came from the crowd of family and friends. Sarah stood speechless, holding Josephine Charlotte's slender hand in hers. Then she dropped it and whirled around to her father, her white satin gown

154

shining silver in the moonlight.

"Papa, how *could* you? Before all these people!" she cried. "Just as though she were a *horse!*"

She burst into a flood of tears and ran sobbing across the lawn and into the house.

chapter 16

"I CAN'T DO IT, Harry. I just simply cannot do it!"
Sarah declared emphatically.

Josephine Charlotte was putting Miss Sarah's
clothes away in the front bedroom upstairs in Mr.
Harry's small house. She heard Miss Sarah's voice
ending on a rising note of distress, and wondered what
had preceded it.

"Jo, where are you?" Sarah called.

"Oh no, don't call her now," Mr. Harry protested.
"Wait until we've settled it."

"It is settled," Sarah insisted. "At least as far as I'm
concerned. Jo, can you hear me?"

156

Josephine Charlotte leaned out of the window to answer, "Do you want me?"

"Yes, please come down here for a few minutes," Sarah said.

When Josephine arrived on the veranda where they were sitting, Mr. Harry had gone off, grumbling, to find George and bring him to the conference.

"I want you and George both to hear what I have to say," Sarah explained.

Mr. Harry and George returned together in a moment, and the two young Negroes sat down on the steps to listen.

"Now, Sarah," said Harry, resolutely, "it has to be done, and the longer you delay, the harder it will be. I'm sure Jo would want you to be quick about it, for her own sake."

"But you don't understand, Harry," his bride wailed. "I just can't do it at all. I came to a decision on our wedding night, and I thought you understood, that I simply can't own Josephine Charlotte as my slave. It was wonderful of Papa to give her to me, but I have no intention of filing the papers of ownership he gave me this morning."

There was a dead silence on the veranda. Josephine looked at Mr. Harry and read disbelief in his face. She supposed her own face must mirror the same emotion, for she saw George watching her very intently, with mingled feelings sweeping across his. Mr. Harry was the first to regain his composure.

"I don't believe you have recovered from the fatigue of the wedding yet, my dear," he said in

157

measured tones. "Your emotional response to your papa's announcement of such a generous gift was understandable, but now you must begin to control your feelings. Jo's welfare demands that you make every possible arrangement for a happy future for her."

Sarah stood up and walked back and forth on the veranda, tossing her golden curls in the sunlight.

"That's just what I'm trying to do, Harry," she said. "I intend to see that she has a future of her own, and not just mine. I thought you knew."

"Now, my darling," Harry began all over again, drawing her down on the bench beside him, "I want you to calm yourself and think more rationally about this matter that can affect two lives, and yes, even three, so drastically. Think of how fine a thing it was for your father to make it possible for you and Jo to spend the rest of your lives together. How could either one of you be happy separated?"

"I could be very happy separated from her if it meant she could live a free life of her own the way I do."

Her voice was rising again with tension. It was under such conditions that Josephine Charlotte usually stepped in to pour oil on the troubled waters, but this time she didn't know how. It was very evident to her that Mr. Harry was controlling his exasperation with difficulty.

"I want you all to listen to me," he insisted. "Do you really know what is involved for a Negro given freedom?"

He didn't wait for an answer, but hurried on.

"He has no place to go where he can be comfortable or safe, no one to look after him, often no way to earn a decent living. If he stays in the South, he has all sorts of problems, like those poor free Negroes Jo found kidnapped. If he goes North, the problems are different, but still tremendous."

He stopped for breath, but when Sarah tried to break in he raised his hand for silence and plunged on.

"Now, Sarah, and Jo, compare that life with life here in our home. Think what a good life you have here, Jo—friends all around you, people who treat you kindly, your wonderful relationship with Miss Sarah, later on helping her bring up her babies, just as though they were your own. Wouldn't you love that? And best of all," he finished, triumphantly playing his trump card, "you and George can be married just as soon as you like, and live here together all the rest of your lives. Isn't that ideal?"

He stopped speaking and looked hopefully from one to the other of his listeners. Josephine Charlotte looked at Miss Sarah and saw that she was on the verge of tears. It wasn't easy to stand up to your new husband within days of your marriage, especially one so forceful and convincing. He painted such a rosy picture of the life of a slave in his household. But Sarah held out.

"I think I know how Jo feels," she said. "No matter how happy she is with us, she wants to live her own life. I've felt that she wanted to be free ever since she came back from the woods. You do want to be free, don't you, Jo?"

She turned her blue eyes, dark with the deepness of her feeling, upon Josephine Charlotte, but before Jo had a chance to respond, Mr. Harry jumped in again.

"Free?" he exclaimed. "Why, compared with what she has here, that's absurd! She's a very intelligent, sensible girl. You don't want to be free, do you, Jo?"

Josephine Charlotte arose and drew herself up to her full height. She glanced first at George beside her, with an inscrutable look in his eyes; she looked at Miss Sarah, waiting tensely for her response, and then she looked straight at Mr. Harry and answered him softly but with great clarity.

"Yes sir, I do want to be free." And then she found herself saying aloud the words she had repeated over and over again to herself, "No human being should *ever* be owned by another!"

Mr. Harry threw up his hands and turned away; George got up and put his arm protectively around her, and Sarah just sat there with a strange little smile on her lips and in her eyes. Finally she said to her husband,

"Harry, I'd like to have Cousin William here to tell us what to do. May George ride over to Fallston for him?"

"We certainly need *somebody* to tell us what to do," he agreed ruefully. "I think we should send for your papa to talk some sense into you; but if you want Cousin William, I suppose you can have him. Go now, George, and see if you can get back before dinner."

Cousin William dropped his work at home and came. After dinner they all gathered on the veranda once more to talk about Josephine Charlotte's future. Mr. Harry made one more attempt to convince the women, and Jo felt sincerity in his words, even though she knew he was appalled at the thought of his wife's giving up such a valuable gift from her father.

"Jo, think hard before you give the final word. Once Miss Sarah signs a writ of manumission there is no turning back. Think how lonesome you will be away from your home; and, of course, you realize this will mean giving up your marriage to George."

"That's just what I wanted to talk about," Sarah said. "I have the perfect solution. If you give George his freedom, too, at the same time, then they can be married and go up North to live. Wouldn't that be wonderful?"

"Wonderful indeed, my dear," Mr. Harry nodded, "but the only trouble with it is that frankly I can't afford to give George his freedom. Do you have any idea how much he's worth? I paid John Thompson eight hundred, and I could ill afford it. If I were a man of means, I would gladly give him his freedom, but I can't."

Cousin William had been sitting quietly listening to the talk, a faraway, thoughtful look in his eyes. Now he began to speak,

"As I see it, there is no problem as far as Jo's being manumitted is concerned. She wants her freedom, and Sarah wants her to have it. The problem lies in her relationship with George. They want to be married, but Harry feels he can't afford to let him go; hence, if Josephine and George are ever to be married, we shall have to work out some solution to this."

"Harry, do you realize you are just *inviting* George to run away?" Sarah broke in. "Every time the newspaper comes out there's an ad for some poor slave who ran away. I 'spose I shouldn't be talking like this in front of him, but after all we've discussed the whole thing quite openly."

George looked quizzically at Miss Sarah, and then at Mr. Harry.

"Don't worry, I'm not aiming to run away," he said dryly. "I wouldn't relish running the rest of my life, and that's what I'd have to do. If you go to a free state, you can be brought back any time. You couldn't sleep at night for worrying; and if you run as far as Canada, you're still not sure to be safe. What kind of life would that be for Josephine Charlotte? She'd be better off without me."

Jo managed to stifle the sob in her throat, but the tears welled up in her eyes and ran unheeded down her cheeks. George put his arms around her and whispered,

"Don't cry, darling. Please don't cry. I can't stand it!"

Cousin William cleared his throat and blew his nose and said, huskily,

"I don't think the situation is as bleak as it may appear. I have a plan for Jo. In Philadelphia there is a Quaker family, close friends of mine, who often help Negroes who are manumitted or, well, are otherwise

162

on their way north. With thy permission I shall get in touch with them and ask if Jo can stay there as long as it's mutually agreeable. They will let her work for her keep, and not demand too much of her, I'm sure, so she should be able to earn money, perhaps with her sewing, to help buy George's freedom." He looked speculatively at Mr. Harry and continued, "Of course, it will take her a long time to earn $800.00, and they will have to wait some years before they can be married; but they're young, and if they love each other enough——" his voice trailed off, and he sat looking out across the lawn to the rolling fields beyond.

A deep red flush started at Mr. Harry's collar and spread up into his face.

"I'm not completely without feeling, William," he exploded angrily. "I certainly wouldn't expect eight hundred for George. I'd be glad to settle for five hundred."

Cousin William beamed while the rest of the people held their breath.

"Of course, thee is not insensitive, son," he soothed. "That's downright handsome of thee to knock off three hundred. Now, if it were possible for George to work for wages somewhere around here, in addition to the work he does for thee?"

Harry hesitated, but only for a fraction of a second, catching the imploring look in his wife's tearful eyes.

"Of course," he agreed, "that could be arranged, I'm sure. Men are always looking for extra help, and I have to say George is a good worker. There isn't much he can't do, indoors or out."

"Now I think we have the solution we've been looking for, my children," Cousin William said urbanely. He got up and held out his hands to them. "I must go home now. A friend of our Meeting in Fallston is leaving for Philadelphia on the morning stage. I shall send a letter to my friends there about Josephine Charlotte. He will bring us a reply when he returns next week. Thee should be on thy way soon, my dear. In the meantime, Sarah, thee must file these papers in Bel Air so that thee will be able to sign her writ of manumission. Thee won't mind filing the ownership papers, knowing it is necessary if thee is to grant her freedom, will thee? Harry will know how to help thee with all the details. It is really quite simple."

In a few minutes he had ridden out of sight on his tall gray horse, leaving Josephine Charlotte feeling as though she were living in some kind of fantasy. She was to have her freedom; it had all happened so fast. It seemed to her only a few short days had passed since she was a happy, carefree little girl, secure with Miss Sarah in Master Robert's house, her troubles the transitory ones of any girl growing into womanhood. Now she had lived through experiences so shattering that, casting aside the remnants of her old life, she had pitched headlong into the new, in some ways ill-prepared for what she might find there.

She went about her familiar tasks for Miss Sarah. She helped Aunt Melissy in the kitchen and around the house. But she lived for the evening hours when, the day's work done, she and George could sit alone in the dusk. They cherished every minute of the time left to them. She had apprehensions about the coming years that struck very deep within her, but they were stilled by the feel of his arms about her as they talked.

They sat thus the first evening in August. A neighbor of Cousin William's had delivered a letter from him that afternoon saying that the Quaker family would be delighted to have her stay with them, that she could work for her keep, and as he had told her, they would see to it that she had extra time to earn money besides. They could promise as much sewing as she could do. She had awaited that word eagerly, but perversely, now that it had come, she was terribly upset. The parting time, so near at hand, seemed more than she could bear at the moment. Cousin William's letter had also contained the news that he intended to see her safely to Philadelphia himself, that he wouldn't think of letting her go alone, but they must set out very soon so he could be back by the end of the month. They would go on horseback, Josephine Charlotte riding his chestnut.

"I wish I knew how much money I can earn, sewing," she said wistfully. "I wish I knew how long it will be before I have earned enough and we can be together always."

"You aren't going to be doing it alone, Jo," he reminded her.

He pulled a dollar out of his pocket and laid it in her lap.

"See," he tried to cheer her, "I earned this working for Master Andrews today, and he was very pleased with me. He can use me any time I can spare him a few hours."

Josephine Charlotte looked at the dollar in the folds of her gown and burst into tears.

"Why darling," he exclaimed in dismay, "I thought you'd be pleased. That's why I showed it to you."

"I am pleased," she sobbed, "but you worked for hours and hours, and I know you're tired, and it's such a little bit. We have to have five hundred of them!"

"I'm all rested now," he insisted, turning her face up to his. "Look at me—do I look tired? Every bit of money I earn will be put away for my manumission, and you will be able to save quite a bit, too, although you'll have expenses that I don't have, and in just no time at all——", his voice died away with the sentence hanging in mid-air.

"In no time at all," she repeated after him. "Oh George, you know better than that! Now that we know it's to be so soon, I almost think I can't do it!"

"Is there any other way out?" George asked quietly. "You could stay here, and we could be married; but you have been very determined that you don't want to be married in slavery."

She stirred uneasily in his arms. "No," she murmured. "I don't want that."

"Besides," George went on, "there's Miss Sarah and her feelings. If she can't bear to have you for a slave, what else could you do? Would you like to go back to Uphill Farm and be maid to Miss Mary Ann or Miss Ellen?"

"Dear heaven, no!" Josephine Charlotte exclaimed.

166

"They've been nice to me since I came back, but not that, anyhow."

Suddenly she was laughing and crying together, clinging to him, groping desperately for the courage to do what she must do.

"No, I'll go to Philadelphia, and we'll both work and save; and it won't be so long, will it, my dearest? It won't be so long!"

Josephine Charlotte worked steadily through the next week, resolutely avoiding every emotional situation that she could. She put all of Miss Sarah's wardrobe in order, everything pressed and mended and hung neatly away. She washed and ironed her own meager belongings and made ready to go. Miss Sarah rode into Bel Air one morning with Mr. Harry. When they returned, her eyes were red and swollen. She went at once to her room, and Josephine Charlotte found her standing by the window when she followed her. Sarah turned and looked at her intently for a long moment, and then she took a folded paper from her handbag and held it out to her.

"Here it is," she managed to say clearly before her voice failed her, and she flung herself into Josephine Charlotte's arms as she had during so many moments of stress all her life.

"Jo, I love you so much. I *do* want you to be free, but how can I bear it to let you go away from me— so far away, to Philadelphia?" she sobbed.

Josephine held the paper in one hand and smoothed Sarah's golden hair with the other, afraid to trust her voice. It would be intolerable if she cried, too.

"Aren't you going to read it?" Sarah faltered. "I want you to."

"I don't think I'd better try right now," Jo murmured.

She read it to George that night, sitting with him in the blue twilight.

Negro Josephine

State of Maryland, Harford County to wit,

Hereby certify that the bearer hereof Negro Josephine, five feet six inches high, seventeen years of age, of a dark complexion, several scars on her back, became free on the 8th day of August 1816 in virtue of a deed of manumission made by Sarah Gilbert of said County and duly executed and recorded among the land records of Harford County Court. The said Negro Josephine was raised in said County. In testimony whereof I have hereunto set my hand and affixed the seal of my office this 8th day of August 1816.

IDENTIFIED BY HARRY GILBERT
AS PER AFFIDAVIT FILED

JEFFREY SMITH, *Clerk*

She held it to her lips before she tucked it into the bosom of her gown, and there she carried it every day, close and warm against her breast.

Cousin William came early one morning, in his

168

neat gray traveling clothes, riding on the tall gray horse, leading the chestnut for Josephine Charlotte. Sarah and Mr. Harry came out of the house with her; George was there; and Aunt Melissy came from the kitchen, wiping her hands on her apron. There was nothing more to say, no more tears to be shed in the misty chill of the August dawn. Josephine Charlotte's slight possessions were ready, and George tied them to the side saddle before he lifted her to the chestnut's back. They had said their farewells the night before. Now she sat straight in the saddle, trying to look beyond him, over his head, to avoid the brilliant dark eyes. Only her hand trembled against his; she held her lip steady with her even white teeth.

Sarah came close and lifted her face for Josephine Charlotte to read the agony of sorrow and joy imprinted there. No word passed between them—no words needed to be said. Josephine Charlotte bent her dark head and pressed her lips against Sarah's golden one. In a moment it was over. Sarah turned and fled into the house. Cousin William mounted his horse and raised his hand in farewell. Josephine Charlotte risked one look into George's eyes, and she was gone, riding away from him, north on the misty road.